Four Seasons

Short and Sweet

Annie Seaton

and

Susanne Bellamy

Short and Sweet: 1

Ten Days in Paradise

Annie Seaton

Chapter One

'Stop! Jane, stop right there. What do you think you're doing?'

I took my hand from the door knob and stared at my mother, blinking away the tears that stung my red eyes. I'd cried myself to sleep last night and now the tears were threatening to spill over—again. I knew it was more a self-esteem thing and not really what Brad had done. Knowing that I didn't really care about his deception had been a big wake-up call.

It had been another kick in the self-esteem guts. But no more.

No. I'd decided it was time to pull up my big girl panties and move on. I was leaving. I pushed the errant lock of hair that fell over my face and squared my shoulders to take on my mother for the first time in my life.

Something I should have done a long time ago, and if I had done, I wouldn't be in this embarrassing situation I now found myself in. A wave of prickly heat rose beneath my skin as I thought about the day ahead.

My wedding day.

'Mum, I don't give a flying f—'

'Jane! Language!' Mum's voice was full of exasperation as usual, but I didn't care.

'All right. I don't care *one bit* that everyone is upset. Me calling off the wedding last night isn't the only reason you and Bradley's mother are upset. Just because you and Joanie have been best friends since high school, and thought you were going to be grandmothers together one day, doesn't mean I have to accept what that lying bastard did.'

'Language, Jane!'

'No. I'll say what I want and how I want to say it. I guess you were getting the best part of the deal and that's why you're so upset. You were getting gorgeous Bradley as a son-in-law, and poor Joanie was getting plain Jane.'

Mum placed her perfectly manicured fingers on my arm, but I pulled away. 'Don't be silly, sweetheart. Joanie was so looking forward to taking you shopping and introducing you to her stylist too.'

I rolled my eyes. 'Are you trying to tell me I should go ahead with the wedding to that jerk? So I can have a stylist and go shopping? No way.' I shook my head and this time when my hair fell across my face, my hand shook when I pushed it back.

But it was from anger, not nerves.

'I don't know what he's done to upset you! It can't be that bad. You're just way too sensitive. You always have been,

Jane. You have to toughen up. Bradley is such a gentleman. And, sweetheart, the wedding! Everything is organised. The caterers, the flowers, the accommodation for the guests. Your Uncle Rollo has come all the way from Venice to marry you.' Mum reached to the hall stand for her Ventolin inhaler and I resisted rolling my eyes. She wasn't one bit breathless; it was simply a ploy to gain my sympathy. She had more chance of losing her breath from inhaling the cloying fragrance of the lilies beside her inhaler. 'Every girl gets nervous on her wedding day.'

I shook my head. 'No. It's off and I'm leaving.'

'But darling—' Mum took a puff and reached her other hand out to me again as panic flitted across her face. Good, she was starting to see I was serious.

'I am not marrying Brad Devine. Not today. Not tomorrow. Not ever.'

'Brad's going to be a perfect husband for you. And you are so lucky he chose you.'

'I'm so *lucky*?' My eyes widened as I stared at her in disbelief. 'What? Because I'm plain Jane, and he's the sexy man about town?' My voice was bitter. 'I know he didn't choose me for my looks, and I was stupid enough to believe that he cared about me. Me, the person, not me, the member of the wonderful Sullivan family. It's all about Dad's company and Bradley's precious career.'

'But sweetheart, you looked beautiful at the wedding

rehearsal.'

'And don't think I didn't see the surprise on everyone's face. Even yours, *Mother* dear. Amazing what a bit of makeup and a hairdresser can do, hey?'

I hadn't inherited much in the way of beauty from the family gene pool. Long, lanky limbs, hair neither brown nor blonde, and big eyes in a skinny face. Yep, plain Jane fitted.

'Well, Jane, if you took more pride in your appearance and stopped messing about on boats, not caring how you look or what you wear, you could look attractive all the time.'

My laugh held no mirth. 'You've got it in one. Not beautiful. *Attractive*. Tell me, Mum. Did you call me Jane because I was an ugly baby?'

'Don't be stupid,' she snapped. 'Of course not. Jane was your grandmother's middle name.'

I looked down at the suitcase sitting on the floor next to the door I'd been about to open when Mum heard me creeping out. She'd rushed downstairs in her Dior silk nightie, no makeup and hair loose. Probably the first time anyone had seen Gloria Sullivan less than perfect.

Perfect! Everything in our house, our garden, our lives was perfect. Everything except for me. Plain Jane.

Or it had been perfect until I'd let myself into my future husband's apartment yesterday afternoon, to leave him a surprise before our wedding. Bradley had maintained we couldn't afford a honeymoon until he got the annual bonus from Dad's company at the end of the year, so I'd bought the charter package and airline tickets with the last of my savings.

As a surprise.

A sailing holiday around Deception Island, a small island in the South Pacific. I was determined to teach Brad to love sailing as much as I did. I'd taped our itinerary to a bottle of his favourite merlot, and I'd been going to leave it on the kitchen countertop.

But I was the one who got the surprise, wasn't I? The truth was Brad didn't want to go on a honeymoon with me; it wasn't about the money. I wondered now how he had been going to live in the same house with me.

My eyes had narrowed when I spotted the handbag on the sofa and the stiletto heels lying abandoned outside the bedroom door.

The closed bedroom door.

The merlot ended up in the wheelie bin on the footpath outside his apartment.

I couldn't help the snort I expelled

'What was that for?' Mum's eyes narrowed, and I realised how saggy her eyelids were these days. She wouldn't like that.

'What was what for?' I said.

'The noise you made. That snort. Most unladylike.'

'I don't have time to talk, Mum. I've ordered a taxi.'

'Where are you going? Where will I tell Bradley to find

you?'

'He doesn't need to find me. It's over, Mum.' Heat filled my chest; bile rose up into my throat and more tears threatened. I pushed it back and let the anger consume me; I was usually such a softie and always gave in to keep the peace.

But not this time.

No, not this time, and never again.

Jane Sullivan was a new woman.

A strong woman who was never going to give in to what everyone wanted her to do or be made a fool of again.

Jane Sullivan was going to live the life *she* wanted.

I picked up my suitcase, opened the door and stepped out. The last thing I saw before I left our perfect life was my mother's mouth stuck open like a fish gasping for air.

The door closed behind me with a satisfying thud, and I hurried out to the waiting taxi.

I'd booked two days in a hotel in the city to lick my wounds and then I was off on a ten-day sailing adventure in paradise.

Alone.

Chapter Two

Linc Martin left the administration office on Columbus Island in a foul mood. Deception Island was under the jurisdiction of the larger island; both islands had once been a small territory of Australia and had gained their independence in the nineteen fifties.

It might as well still be the nineteen fifties.

Frustration filled Linc as he made his way to the airport to catch the short island hop that would take him the fifty kilometres across to Deception Island.

A wife! The president had actually called him in to tell him he had found—no, *chosen*—a wife for him. One of his brother's cousin's friend's daughters or some other convoluted relationship. A woman who was apparently a suitable wife for the police chief of Deception Island.

David Kekoa had lowered his imposing bulk into the chair behind his desk and shaken his head. 'I am very happy with your policing work, Lincoln, but I have had some disturbing reports of you socialising a little too much with some of the female tourists on the island.' The president steepled his fingers and looked over his glasses at Linc, his triple chins wiggling as he spoke. 'It will not do. So, I have taken matters in hand and found you a suitable partner.'

Even at thirty-one, Linc had felt like a naughty boy called to the headmaster's office.

'I think that you might find that those reports are greatly exaggerated, David.' He bit back the anger that rose quickly. This was all political; Tommy Kekoa, his deputy and the president's nephew was always undermining him and had his eyes on the chief of police position. And there had been *no* unsuitable socialising; the stories were all Tommy's fabrication. 'While I am very grateful for your concern, David, there is no need for that.' The lie sprang to Linc's lips easily; he knew that David would get his own way unless it was nipped in the bud at the outset. 'Thank you for thinking of me, but I have a girlfriend, and we are planning to get married.'

Tommy Kekoa wasn't above using fair means or foul, so Linc was in a difficult position. Thus, Linc had no hesitation in twisting the truth or he would find a wedding and a wife organised for him before he knew it.

The president's brow furrowed. 'Why did I not know about that?'

Linc had trouble keeping his expression bland. 'She isn't here yet. We have been corresponding for a couple of years, and we met when I was in Australia last Christmas. Love at first sight.' He glanced at the president, wondering if he had gone too far.

'That's wonderful news. I will look forward to meeting this woman very much.' David's eyebrows lifted but Linc held his gaze steadily. 'And soon, Lincoln.'

Linc kept his smile innocent as he shook the president's hand. 'I will bring her over to meet you as soon as she arrives.'

Hell, where was he going to find a woman to masquerade as his future wife? The island was small, and everyone knew everyone else's business there anyway.

As he climbed out of the taxi at the airport an hour later, he was hailed by a familiar voice. 'Linc!'

Linc turned and his bad mood dissolved when he spotted Johnny Tatua, one of his mates from the island. As much as Tommy might hate him being the police chief, Linc was a local; he'd been born and bred on Deception Island and he had earned the senior position through hard work and study.

'Hey, Johnny. Are you my pilot today?'

'I am, bro. What brings you over to the big island?'

'I was summoned by our president.'

The two friends chatted as they walked into the small terminal, and Johnny laughed when Linc told him about his day.

'We'd better find you a woman and fast,' he said with his usual grin.

Linc looked at him feeling glum. 'Easier said than

done, mate.'

'Come and we'll grab a coffee. The Brisbane flight picked up a tail wind, so the next island hop's been brought forward an hour.' Johnny said. 'That'll only leave half an hour or so between my two flights this afternoon. I'll just about pass myself coming back.'

'Have we got a few tourists coming in?' Linc looked at him hopefully.

'The flight you're on has only got one tourist booked, but the second jet coming in from Brisbane is full.'

'Maybe there's a single woman on it. Someone who's happy to pretend to be my fiancée,' Linc said.

Johnny tapped him on the shoulder. 'I don't like your chances, mate.' His voice was full of mirth. 'What's wrong with one of the president's nieces anyway?'

Linc rolled his eyes. 'Where do I start?

Chapter Three

Jane

When I'd changed the dates on the holiday package and my air tickets online on Friday night, I'd cancelled Brad's ticket, and the extra two thousand dollars that had been credited to my account was all that was between me and starvation. I'd used my credit card to pay for the hotel room while I waited for Monday to arrive.

The holiday package was an expensive luxury charter and I'd booked the yacht for ten days and ordered the gold level food and drink provisioning. It had taken everything I'd had in my savings account.

Stuff it, I'd thought. I might as well keep that and have a good holiday, because when I came back home, I was going to have to find a job.

How stupid had I been to hand over the bulk of my savings to Bradley to put a deposit on our dream house last month? I guess I'd get that back eventually.

Gah. And how stupid had I been to quit my job to "prepare for the wedding"? My mother's words, not mine. I'd loved my job teaching at the sailing club, but I had an excellent reputation and contacts, so I was sure I'd find something. Maybe I'd move further north. I didn't have to stay in Brisbane.

'Have a wonderful trip.' The woman at the check-in counter smiled at me as she handed over my baggage receipt.

The knowledge that no one in the whole world knew where I was going to be for the next couple of weeks while I licked my wounds and figured out what I was going to do, filled me with a sense of unfamiliar freedom. A tentative smile tugged at my mouth as I slung my handbag over my shoulder and headed for the gate.

There were only four other passengers waiting in the lounge on the lower floor of Brisbane Airport. It looked like the two-hour flight to Columbus Island wasn't going to be packed. A young couple sat there watching a small boy play with a car on the carpet at their feet; the woman looked up and smiled at me, and I nodded back. An older man in shorts and a khaki work shirt was engrossed in a newspaper and wasn't even aware that I took the seat opposite him.

I slid my handbag beneath my seat and stared through the window that overlooked the runways. I focused on the freedom that had risen a moment ago, and refused to let any doubts creep in.

I was *not* going to marry a man who slept with my best friend and bridesmaid—my former best friend—the day before we were supposed to promise our lives and love to each other. It had been clear from the giggling and voices coming from behind that closed door exactly what was going on. I'd been naive; when I thought back to the social occasions where Serena always seemed to turn up, I realised that Brad and Serena had always been too touchy-feely for platonic friends.

I didn't care that a mess had been left behind. That could be sorted by Mum and Joanie; after all they'd organised the whole shebang. All I was supposed to do was get dressed in the designer gown, be lathered in makeup and turn up at the church and then dance at the reception.

And you know what?

I didn't care one bit that I wasn't marrying Brad. I'd been railroaded into the engagement and then the wedding by both our families.

You know I can't even recall that Brad ever proposed.

When I was a teenager, I'd read my grandmother's romance novels, and I'd fallen in love with the idea of love.

Love at first sight. That moment when you saw him and knew that this was the man you would love. Back in those days, I'd looked forward to meeting someone who made my heart race, that special someone who looked at me as though I was the most important person in his world. Someone who loved the things that I did, and someone who was happy in my company. A man who wanted me to be happy.

I'd given up on my fairy-tale dream a long time ago. Because Brad had never done any of that, and I'd simply gone with the flow. That's all it had been. There was no such thing as love.

And love at first sight?

Pfft. The stuff of dreams and romance novels.

I sighed as my flight was called.

Think of this as an escape, Jane.

Once I was on the jet I leaned back and rested my head against the cushion as exhaustion overtook me. I hadn't slept for the two nights in the hotel. It wouldn't hurt to close my eyes for a short while now.

It seemed like only minutes later that the flight attendant was shaking my shoulder gently.

'We're about to land, madam. Can you please put your window blind up and bring your seat upright?'

The jet circled the island once and the wheels came down with a bump as we descended. I swallowed; I hated flying, so sleeping for most of the flight had been good. All I had to do now was survive the landing, and the next short flight to Deception Island.

We disembarked, and as I entered the terminal, a voice with a lilting accent announced that the flight to Deception Island had been delayed by an hour. My luggage was booked through so all I had to do was head to the transit lounge and wait for the flight to be called.

Holding my boarding pass, I walked across to the coffee lounge and queued behind two tall men, before I ordered my coffee. I dug into my pocket and pulled out the ten dollar note that I'd put in there earlier to save digging my wallet out of my bag. The men were speaking loudly, and it was hard not to listen to their conversation. I don't think they realised there was anyone behind them. I shrugged and tried to switch off. They were obviously locals as they had the same lilting accent as the speaker over the PA system.

'So, you've been nightclubbing with the lady tourists again,' the man in the white shirt said.

'You know me. I can't help myself,' the other one replied.

'You've always loved the ladies, Linc. Just as well he's going to marry you off.'

The second man chuckled, and he had an attractive deep laugh, but their conversation unsettled me. 'No, he can't. I told him I have a fiancée all lined up to keep him happy.'

'Do I know this mystery woman?'

'No, but the funny thing is, neither do I. I haven't got one yet.'

'We'll go through my phone contacts. We've got time.'

Disgust curled in my stomach.

Men. They were the same the world over.

I stepped forward as they moved away with their coffees and the man who was supposedly searching for a fiancée stared at me. A strange tingling zinged through my nerve endings and I frowned,

'Don't even think about it, buddy,' I thought.

I was done with men for life. There was no such thing as love or Cupid's arrow.

As I stood there waiting for my double shot espresso, I dreamed of buying a boat and sailing the world by myself.

Ten minutes later I was still dreaming of sailing into the wild blue yonder as I stood at the observation window watching the planes on the tarmac below.

'No, not that one. Red and white isn't a good look.' The familiar voice came from behind me and I recognised the first coffee man's voice without turning around.

I glanced down at my red jeans and white polo top with the sailing club insignia on the pocket.

Who the hell did he think he was?

'And she's way too heavy at the arse end,' came the voice of the man whose good looks had sent that tingle through me

What the—? Humiliation washed over me. I froze; there was no way I was going to turn around and let them know I'd heard every word they said. Okay, I knew I was thin, but I was out of proportion in the boobs and hips department. Brad had often told me I had an interesting shape.

Interesting!

I backed into a seat and sat down heavily on my wider than acceptable "arse end" and sipped my coffee until the embarrassment passed and my face had cooled.

Finally, the flight to Deception Island was called, and

when I stood there was no sign of either of them.

I slipped my handbag over my shoulder and headed for the gate. The stewardess smiled at me, and the coloured flowers woven into her dark hair bobbed as she nodded at my boarding pass. The cigar-shaped plane was so small I had to bend down as I walked along the aisle to my seat in the second back row.

Oh no. I hesitated as I approached my allocated seat. The good looker from the coffee lounge was sitting across the aisle from my seat. He gave me a huge smile, and I would have smiled back if it hadn't been for the conversation I'd overheard. Not to mention the comment about my fat rear end.

Of course, he was good-looking; that usually went with the confidence and the sexist attitude. So, I raised my eyebrows and stared at him without acknowledging his smile and then slid into my seat, working up my courage to survive the take-off, the short flight ahead and the landing. I leaned back, folded my arms and closed my eyes. Within a couple of hours, I would be on the water—in my comfort zone—happily ensconced on the yacht I had hired for ten days.

Gold provisioning. Caviar, seafood and Moet champagne. I pulled a face.

What a waste by myself.

The propellers began to spin, the motors vibrated, and that uneasy feeling settled in the pit of my stomach.

Almost there, Jane. You can do it.

Maybe I could get a job on the island, and I wouldn't have to face the flights back. I nodded to myself thoughtfully. That wasn't such a bad idea; I'd heard about the huge international marina on Deception Island, with privately-owned boats, and a few different companies chartering boats for the trips around the islands. There was a cluster of small islands and coral atolls between Deception and Columbus Islands. I'd had fun choosing the luxury sailboat for our holiday.

Anger with a slight tinge of disappointment mixed to settle in my stomach again and it stayed there as the small plane droned on towards our destination.

It was a bad time for the guy across the aisle to reach over and touch my arm—not that any time would have been good. I looked at him as though he had crawled out from beneath a rock, but he kept that damn happy smile on his face.

'If you look down now, you'll be able to see Deception Island.'

'Thank you.' No matter what sort of mother Gloria was, she had drummed good manners into me. I nodded and did as requested, leaning over and looking down. The water was sapphire blue and as the plane banked to the left, I could see the small white caps on the ocean below.

The island came into view, and I was surprised by how small it was. A township ran along the front of the lagoon, and up to the foothills of the extinct volcanoes I'd read about in the tourist brochures. At the northern end I could see the boats in the marina. At each end of the island, the sides of the two mountains were covered in lush green forest and on the eastern side, a lagoon was fringed by reef where the breakers were spewing white foam into the air. My mood improved as happy anticipation kicked in. A good sea was running. Excellent— that meant wind, and wind meant good sailing.

The plane shuddered and dropped a little during the descent and I swallowed and gripped the arm rests.

Yep, a job on the island was a real possibility.

'It's okay.' The voice from across the aisle was soothing and again I felt that strange tingle. 'We always get strong crosswinds between the two mountains. Johnny's one of the best pilots around. They don't let many pilots take this flight. The runway's extra short too, and passengers always think we'll end up in the surf on the other side of the island. You watch how smartly Johnny pulls us up.'

'Thanks,' I said drily. 'I can't wait.'

'Your first visit to the island?' he persisted.

Again, I nodded, but didn't engage this time.

'Where are you staying?'

I straightened in the small seat and this time I curled my lip as I stared back at him. 'Is that any of your business?'

'I'm sorry.' At least he had the decency to look contrite. 'Please don't think I was asking because I have an ulterior motive.' He held his hand out across the aisle. 'I'm

Linc Martin. I'm the police chief on Deception Island. And I can assure you that you'll be safe on our island.'

'Really?' My voice was so cold it was a wonder there weren't icicles forming on the plane. 'I thought someone in your position would have better manners.'

'Manners?' His brow wrinkled in a frown. 'I'm sorry if I've offended you by chatting.'

'Oh, no. You offended me before that,' I said as he stared at me. All the anger that I had held inside since yesterday bubbled up and the handsome police chief wore the tirade that Bradley, Serena, and even my mother and Joanie deserved. Heat rose up my neck and burned my cheeks as the words spewed out. 'Okay, you want to know how you offended me?' There was no stopping now that I'd let go. 'One, I didn't appreciate being dismissed because of my choice of clothes and two, because I have a fat arse. No, I don't mean being dismissed, I mean I don't want to be considered anyway. It was what you said about me that I found rude and offensive.'

His mouth dropped open. Even through the haze of my anger I couldn't help noticing his even white teeth and perfectly formed lips. And the blue eyes set in the tanned face were unusual—not pale, and not dark. Just a clear intense blue, deepened by the lush dark lashes that surrounded them.

That damn tingle turned into butterflies low in my stomach.

I looked away as I realised we'd been staring at each other for a full minute. Or rather I was glaring, and he was staring at me with a totally confused look on his face.

'Honestly, I have no idea what you're talking about, but if I have offended you in any way, please believe me it was unintentional, and I do apologise.' His smile was gentle, and it got those blasted butterflies fluttering again. I held that gaze and carried on some more.

'Unintentional? So, you're a liar too. Show me a man who's not.' I folded my arms and looked back at him.

The wheels hit the tarmac and, closing my eyes, I braced for the sudden stop. At least I hoped the plane would stop; I didn't like the thought of ending up in the ocean. My seatbelt held me firm as the speed slowed dramatically, but at least I was safely on the ground.

'A liar? May I ask what you are referring to specifically?' His voice was tight and when I opened my eyes the pleasant smile had disappeared. I knew he was holding his temper in. 'Wait a minute, you're not related to David, are you?' His brow creased in a frown.

I lifted my chin. 'David who?'

'David Kekoa, the president.'

'Of course not. How would I know the president and what's he got to do with this anyway?'

'David's the one who was going to find me a wife. I thought for a moment that might have been you. You never know with him; he's got relatives all over the place. That's why I was looking for a pretend fiancée. He's already got someone lined up for me.' His eyes narrowed. 'Anyway, how did you know all this? The only person I've told was Johnny.'

I almost started to feel sorry for him and then I remembered the "arse end" comment. I lifted my chin a bit higher.

'It was a bit hard not to know about it, waiting for my coffee at the airport. Talking to your friend as though you wanted the world to know or maybe you were hoping some poor woman would overhear and come running? You might as well have taken an ad out in the paper. It didn't look like you were too worried about privacy.'

'Eavesdroppers never hear any good of themselves,' he said, and my temper burred up even more.

'I wasn't eavesdropping.' My voice was too loud, and I lowered it. 'I was waiting for my coffee. And how could I not help hearing what you said about my red jeans and white T-shirt when you were standing right behind me.'

The door of the plane opened and the few passengers ahead of us stood and began to make their way out. I sat and waited for his apology, but the last thing I expected was the deep laugh that erupted from those attractive lips.

I looked at him one more time, and then picked up my bag with a final withering glance in his direction, stood and marched down the aisle.

Well, as much as one could march, hunched over in a small plane.

And you know what I was most worried about?

And that made me even crankier.

I was worried that he was sitting there laughing at me and staring at my fat rear end in my tight red jeans.

Chapter Four

Linc waited until the woman in the red jeans was off the plane and crossing the tarmac before he unclipped his seat belt. If she ditched the attitude and smiled, she'd be even prettier. Her face was delicate with high cheekbones and green eyes that tipped up at the corners. She had an unusual beauty and he'd found it hard to stop staring at her.

He'd first noticed her exquisite face when he'd turned around at the airport coffee shop on Columbus Island, but when he'd smiled at her, she'd looked at him and turned away. No wonder if she'd overheard their conversation. He'd been too focused on talking to Johnny to give it a second thought. Linc made his way to the front of the plane and tried to remember what they'd actually said about fake engagements. As much as he had a problem with David wanting to find him a wife, the conversation with Johnny had been light-hearted, but they'd obviously offended her with their levity.

Linc grinned as he stuck his head into the cockpit; an apology was in order.

And fast.

He had to find her and explain; he realised now that she'd overheard them talking about the new plane that David had ordered for government travel. Red and white and a cumbersome shape; the poor woman had thought they were talking about her.

Oh. Jeez.

'What are you looking so stressed about?' Johnny looked up from the flight manifest on his lap. 'Still worrying about finding a wife?'

'Nothing. Or rather something I have to do. Just a misunderstanding I have to sort. I'll catch you later. Have you got time for a drink before you head home tonight?'

'Sounds like a plan to me. Joanna's got a book club meeting at our house, so I was going to ask you to meet me at the hotel.'

'Good stuff. What time does the next flight come in?'

'I'm taking off as soon as I refuel and coming back within the hour. I'll meet you at the bar at six. Suit you?'

'Yeah, I'll go to the station first and see what sort of damage Tommy's caused today.'

'See ya there at six.'

Linc gave Johnny a wave before heading out of the plane. He hurried across the tarmac; he wanted to make sure that he caught up with the woman and explained the misunderstanding. The apology was priority one before the station.

She was scrabbling through her bag at the customs desk. As he walked over, she bent down and tipped the contents of her bag onto the floor. A tube of lipstick rolled towards him and he bent and picked it up.

'Bloody, bloody h—' She muttered cutting off the last word as he crouched down beside her and held out the lipstick.

'Everything okay?' he asked.

'No.' She rifled through the papers and assorted stuff on the floor.

'Can I help?'

After she had pushed everything back into the bag, he held out a hand to help her up, and was surprised when she took it. Her hand was cold, and it was dwarfed by his. He let go of it immediately she was upright.

Putting her bag on the counter, she ran a hand through her hair. 'The only thing I can think of was, it fell out when my bag tipped over at Brisbane Airport.' Her eyes were bleak as she looked up at Jennifer behind the customs desk. Linc had noticed her beauty but not how tiny this woman was when he'd first seen her in the coffee shop.

'What have you lost?' he asked.

'My passport, the booking details for my holiday and all the money I had in the folder.'

His police brain kicked in. 'Could it have been stolen? Did you leave your bag unattended at all?'

She shook her head. 'No. I'm always careful when I travel.'

'Okay. Look. Before I help you sort this, I have to

apologise to you.'

She waved a dismissive hand. 'You're the least of my worries.'

'No, please listen to me and then we'll start again.' Linc took a deep breath. 'When Johnny—he's the guy I was talking to, and the pilot of our plane—when he and I were talking, we weren't talking about you. Honestly, I didn't even see you there. We were talking about the red and white plane on the tarmac. You must have seen it? It's the president's new plane, and if there's one thing about David, he rarely takes advice from anyone. He bought this Russian-designed plane and it's not a good aerodynamic design.' He grinned at her. 'It's heavy in the rear end.'

Her mouth dropped open and she stared at him. Then her eyes crinkled, and she burst out laughing. 'Oh my God, I was so rude to you. You must think I'm crazy. I'm sorry I snapped at you.'

'I don't. I can understand how you thought that. Let's start again.' He held out his hand. 'I'm Linc Martin, police chief of Deception Island.'

She took his hand and as she shook it a tingle ran up his arm. 'Hello, Linc, I'm Jane Sullivan, a hapless tourist who was hoping to have a holiday on your beautiful island.' Her eyes were sad as she continued. 'But I guess without a passport or any form of ID or any money, I won't be staying long.' She looked up at the departures board. 'There's another flight in from Columbus Island in half an hour. I wonder if there's another flight back to Brisbane tonight.'

Linc kept hold of her hand. 'No, the next flight in is the last one for the day. There's no return flight until tomorrow afternoon. But let's not be hasty.' He turned to Jennifer who was manning the custom's desk. 'I'm going to take Ms Sullivan into the office and try to sort this.'

'No problem, Linc.' Jennifer replied and then turned to Jane. 'I'm sure things will work out. Linc will get you sorted. If anyone can help, he'll be able to.'

Linc realised he was still holding Jane's hand when she replied. It was small and warm, and her fingers had curled around his.

'Excellent. I really don't want to have to leave.'

He dropped her hand and gestured for Jane to follow him to the glass-fronted office opposite the customs counter. He paused and dug into his pocket for some coins. 'Jen, could you grab us a couple of bottles of water from the machine, please. We could be a while.'

Jane followed him across to the office where there were two comfortable sofa chairs and a low table. He gestured to the one facing the terminal and waited for her to sit before he settled into the other chair.

'Now, tell me exactly what happened. Where were you when you think you lost your documents?'

'I was sitting in the departure lounge at Brisbane

Airport. Do you know the one down on the bottom level where the island flights leave from?'

He nodded. 'I know where you mean.'

'I was a bit distracted and I put my bag under the seat when I sat down; I didn't think to check if anything had fallen out when I left the seat. It must have happened then, because I had the folder when I checked in. I stuck the baggage claim sticker in the side and then I put it in my bag and didn't take it out again.'

'Okay. I'm going to give Brisbane Airport a call. Don't worry, with a bit of luck it will still be under the seat.'

'Oh, God, I hope so.' Jane sighed and her lips quivered. Linc couldn't take his eyes off her pretty mouth. 'There was two thousand dollars in the folder. I feel so stupid.'

He handed her one of the bottles of water. 'Here you go. Have a drink and try to relax.'

Half an hour later, Linc was still on hold. He'd been transferred from desk to desk and when he'd finally reached the attendant in the departure lounge he required, the call had dropped out before he could speak. He then had to go through the whole transfer process again. Jane sat there fighting agitation as he made the call again.

He glanced at his watch; it was almost five-thirty. If he didn't get through soon, that gate would be closed for the night. He'd caught the last flight out of Brisbane often enough to know the times well. The last flight from that gate left at five-forty five.

As he waited on hold, he heard the drone of the island hopper flight coming to a stop outside the terminal; he'd have to catch Johnny on his way in and take a rain check on their drink.

'Gate Thirty, Andre speaking. How can I help you?'

'Hello. My name is Lincoln Martin and I'm police chief on Deception Island.' Linc gave a thumbs up to Jane and her expression brightened as he spoke quickly explaining what he wanted and describing where Jane had told him which seat she'd been in.

'Just one moment, I'll go and look.'

Linc turned to Jane. 'They're checking now, just cross your fingers the call doesn't drop out again.'

She grinned at him and crossed the fingers on both hands as she held his gaze. Eventually, he looked away as warmth settled in his chest; he could drown in those eyes.

The door to the tarmac slid open and twenty or so tourists headed into the terminal. Jennifer waited at the customs desk ready for the influx.

'We're going to have to wait until the crowd clears now.' Linc nodded to the group coming through the doors.

'Are you there?' Andre's voice pulled his attention back to the call.

'I'm here. How did you go?'

'Yes, all good. The folder was still there under the seat

you described. Can you please give me the name of the passport holder? I'll also need some identification details. Once confirmed, I can fax or email a copy through to you.'

'Just one moment.' Linc said. He handed his phone to Jane with a smile. 'They've found it and need some details from you. His name is Andre.'

'Oh, thank you.' The sweetest smile lifted her lips. 'I owe you.'

He raised his eyebrows. 'Careful, I might hold you to that.'

'Hello, Andre. Can I ask first is my money still there? Okay, I understand. You can't tell me until you have ID. Fair enough.' As Jane gave her details over the phone, Linc watched the tourists queueing at the customs desk.

'Yes, fourteenth of August, '95,' she said. 'No. I don't know the passport number. Yes, I'll ask him. We won't get disconnected, will we? Hang on. I'll get him to use my phone. Linc?'

Linc had been watching one couple in the queue. The guy's hands had been roaming over the woman beside him, and then he'd taken her in a tight clinch and kissed her. Some people have no idea, he thought, shaking his head.

As Jane put his phone down on the low table and dug in her bag, Linc caught sight of the flight crew walking across from the plane. He kept one eye on them; he'd catch Johnny and take a rain check on that drink.

'What's up?' he asked Jane, stifling a groan when he saw who was walking beside Johnny.

'He wants me to text a photo of myself so he can match my photo on my passport for more ID.' She pulled out a phone, smaller than his and used her thumb to scroll through the screen before handing it to him. 'He won't give me any details until he gets the photo. Here use mine, so yours doesn't get disconnected.'

She smiled when Linc lifted the phone to take a shot.

'Don't smile,' he said. 'Not if it's got to look like your passport photo.'

He grinned as Jane tried to compose her face into a serious expression.

'Sorry, I'll do it again. Be quick.' She stared at the camera and he clicked off a shot. 'Hang onto my phone, I'll ask him what mobile number to text it to.' Her smile crumpled as she lifted Linc's phone to her ear. 'Oh, no! The call's dropped out again.'

'Damn. Pass it over and I'll call again.'

Jane took her phone back and held onto it as Linc dialled Brisbane Airport. As he waited for the call to connect, he caught the eye of the Romeo in the queue. His instincts kicked in as the guy's eyes widened as he stared back at Linc. He turned quickly to the woman beside him and she looked over at Linc and horror filled her expression.

What are they up to and how did he know he was

police?

He watched as the woman took off towards the restroom and the guy stayed in the queue. Neither of them looked familiar, and he usually had a pretty good memory for faces. They were up to something, and he was suspicious.

Drugs maybe? Jennifer was pretty laidback when it came to checking luggage. He'd spoken to her about being more vigilant a few times.

'Jane. Can you wait here, please? And when they answer, ask for Andre at gate 30.' He handed her the phone and stood. He'd catch Johnny at the same time.

Jane gasped as she looked past him. 'Oh, God. No!'

Before Linc could turn around to see what she was looking at, she threw the phone onto the table and jumped up beside him. She grabbed at his hands and her expression was stricken. 'Linc. Listen to me! Please? I'll do anything if you help me out. I'll be your pretend fiancée, anything, if you follow my lead. But first, quick, put your arms around me and kiss me.'

Chapter Five

Linc didn't hesitate. Before I knew it, his arms were around me and his lips were against mine. He was tall, and his body was firm and muscled. I wasn't used to that. Brad spent most of his time at the office or at business drinks, and his body was soft.

'I'll explain later,' I murmured into warm lips. Being held tight against that rock-hard chest was very pleasant. I could have stayed there forever.

'I'll look forward to it.' His lips vibrated against mine, and his arms pulled me even closer. 'I just want to turn us around so I can watch someone who was acting suspiciously. Just follow my lead.' He shuffled us around so that he was facing out to the terminal, and my face was blocked from view and that was a relief because I couldn't see Brad anymore.

Yes, Brad!

I'd almost died when I'd looked past Linc and spotted Brad in the queue.

How much worse could this day get?

What the hell was my ex-fiancé doing on Deception Island? How did he find out where I was going? I hadn't told a soul.

The pressure of Linc's lips lessened and he pulled away, although I was still totally shielded from Brad's view.

'We're about to get company,' he said. 'He must have seen me checking him out. Interesting. *Very* interesting; he's on the front foot, that's for sure. And oh, damn. Sorry. More company.'

'What? Who?' I almost screeched. 'He saw me?'

'He?' Linc looked over my head. 'Who's he?'

'You're looking for a fiancée,' I said crossly. 'And I have an ex-fiancé. And that's him walking over here. Just follow my lead. *Please*.'

Before Linc could answer the door opened and Brad pushed into the room closely followed by two men.

'Jane. What are you doing here?' I'd never noticed how bland his voice was before.

'Doing where?' I peeked over Linc's shoulder. One of the men behind Brad was the pilot who'd been in the coffee shop.

'Here. On Deception Island.'

'More to the point what are you doing here?' I demanded.

Linc leaned down and whispered in my ear. 'He's not here alone. Until he saw you, he was with a woman. I thought he was watching me, but he'd obviously spotted you.'

'Hello, hello, hello,' interrupted the huge man beside Linc's mate. He was rubbing his hands together and a wide grin stretched across his plump face. 'I assume this is your lady, Lincoln?'

'Yes, it is David.' Linc's hand pressed into my side and I sensed it was a warning nudge. 'Would you like to have a drink with us? We were about to head to the bar.'

'That would be excellent. Come on, Jonathon, we'll leave these lovebirds in peace and go and order some drinks. I think champagne may be in order?'

Linc nodded and didn't speak, but I could feel the tension in his body beside me.

'Don't be too long,' the man boomed.

Brad frowned as they left the small room. 'I … um … I'm here looking for you,' he stuttered.

'And Serena is helping you? How thoughtful.' My voice was as sweet as honey as I guessed who was with him. 'I don't believe you, Brad.'

'Um, yes she came to help me look for you too.' Brad was sweating and he kept looking over his shoulder.

Linc leaned down and whispered in my ear again. His breath was warm and sent goose bumps down my back. 'You might like to know that he was kissing her in the customs queue.'

'I'm not one bit surprised.' I straightened in Linc's arms and pointed a finger at Brad. 'Tell the truth for the first time in your life.'

'You tell me why you ran away from me, Jane. On our

wedding day.'

'Because I realised, I don't love you. I love Linc and we're engaged.'

The look on his face was comical. 'What? Who's Linc? Is that what that fat guy was talking about.'

'I am.' Linc moved one of his arms from around me and held out a hand to Brad. 'How do you do. I'm Linc Martin, chief of police and Jane's fiancé. And I don't know that our president would appreciate being referred to as the fat guy.'

'But, but—' Brad's Adam's apple moved up and down as he spluttered.

Most unattractive.

I'd never been more pleased than this instant that we'd agreed not to sleep together until we were married. Although since Friday night I'd realised Brad had wanted it that way because his sexual interests lay elsewhere. I'd put it down to me not being attractive enough, but I was starting to wake up to myself. I also knew that I hadn't been keen. Confidence filled me now as I realised how much Brad had impacted on my self-esteem over the last year.

'I think your girlfriend is looking for you,' Linc said.

I looked over his shoulder and sure enough, Serena was standing behind a large potted palm in the terminal looking over at the office.

'Stay there, Jane. I'll be right back.' Brad almost ran

out of the small office and Linc put his arms around me again. 'I'll tell her I found you.'

I couldn't help the chuckle that rose from my chest.

'Are you okay?' Linc put his arms around me and put his cheek against mine. Just to make it look good, I told myself. Not because he was enjoying the contact as much as I was.

'Actually,' I said with a nod, 'I'm the best I've been for a long time. You'd better tell me what's going on before we go and join your friends for a drink. Did you say that man was the *president*?'

'He is. That's David Kekoa.' Linc looked down at me and nodded as I grinned up at him.

'It looks like I've got myself another fiancé. I wonder if that's a record. Two in the same week,' I said.

'And it looks like I have a fiancée.' His deep voice sent a shiver down my back again. 'I'm happy to help you, and I'll be forever grateful if you'll help me out. Now you'd better bring me up to speed on what's been going on, so I don't put my foot in it.'

By the time Brad and Serena slunk into the office—note, they stood metres apart—I had given Linc a two-minute potted history of what had happened, how Brad was only marrying me because of his job with Dad's company and how I'd fled from Brisbane because I'd sprung him with Serena.

'But he doesn't know I did,' I whispered. 'They had no

idea I was in the apartment. I went home, packed my bags and ended up here. And I've no idea why they are here either, or how they even knew I was here. It doesn't make sense. Why would he bring Serena if they knew I was here?'

'You know what? I think it might be a coincidence. The look of horror on their faces doesn't go with the thought that they were expecting to see you here. It wasn't that I was kissing you that shocked them, it was seeing you in the first place. You were the shock to them.'

'So he's brought Serena away for a holiday while he plans his next move.' I made a sound of disgust. 'Her father's well off too.'

'What a jerk.' Linc held me close. 'You're better off without him.'

'I know that now,' I whispered. 'I honestly didn't tell anyone I was coming to Deception Island.'

'No-one?' His breath tickled my ear again as he whispered back.

'Not a soul,' I said. 'Not even my bridesmaid, Serena!'

'Leave it to me.' Linc hugged me and it was a very nice place to be.

***

Linc

Jane stayed close to Linc as her ex and his girlfriend

43

came back into the office. He was now certain that the look of horror hadn't been because of him, but because they hadn't been expecting to see Jane on the island.

He knew Jane still thought that they were here looking for her, but he was about to get them to admit the truth.

I'm not in the police force for nothing, Linc thought as the blonde gripped her hands nervously in front of her.

'Hello, Serena. I'm Linc. Welcome to Deception Island.'

She nodded nervously and glanced at Jane who was holding onto his hand.

'I guess you were absolutely gobsmacked to see Jane here with me, weren't you?'

Serena looked up at the sleaze nervously, as if to ask how are we going to play this?

He *was* a sleaze. Any man who could do the dirty on the woman he was supposed to marry, would get no respect from him.

'Tell me. Why did you pick our island?' Linc asked

'What do you mean *our* island?' Brad interjected. 'I mean, why is it Jane's too?'

'Because she's here to marry me, aren't you, sweetheart.' Linc dropped a kiss on her lips as Jane looked up at him. She was a good actress; the look in her eyes was spot on. Even Linc found it easy to believe she was in love with him.

'But she was supposed to marry me, and she took off.' The sleaze scowled. 'How dare you, Jane! You've been leading me along the whole time.'

'What's good for the goose and all that.' Linc grinned at him. 'Jane told me she knew about you and Serena all along. She was just waiting to see if you'd go through with the wedding. I guess you were going to protect your job along with your future. I guess you thought you could be married, get your hands on Jane's father's money and have Serena on the side.' Linc shook his head. 'Not the way of a gentleman, Brad. Not at all. It's called having your cake and eating it too.'

'What money?' Serena burst into tears. 'I'm sorry, Jane. I didn't mean to hurt you. I love Brad, but he always promised me he would tell you he couldn't marry you. He's always loved me. It killed me to lie to you.'

'Lucky you, Serena.' Jane stepped forward and her voice was calm. 'The sooner you realise you can't believe a word that comes out of his mouth, the better off you'll be. Just make sure he doesn't have a business meeting with your dad.'

Linc pointed to the customs desk. 'I suggest if you two want a holiday here, you go and get yourselves processed. The shuttle bus for the hotel will leave as soon as everyone has been through customs. They don't wait. And we don't have taxis on our island. We might see you around the island while you're here.'

Chapter Six

Jane

Brad's mouth hung open as he stared at me, and Serena stood there looking as though she didn't know what to do.

'Come on, Janey-girl. Let's go get your luggage and then join David and Johnny for that celebratory champagne.' Linc held my hand tightly and we walked out of the office over to the baggage claim area, leaving Brad and Serena staring after us.

Linc leaned down to me. I was getting quite used to him speaking to me up close and personal. 'We'll sort out your passport and money later. At least we know it's safe at the Brisbane Airport. Don't say anything about losing it to David.'

'Can I really leave?' I asked. 'Or what I mean to say is, leave the airport. Can I stay on the island? I haven't got a passport, I haven't been through customs, and I've only got about five dollars in my pocket. And I was so stressed I'd even forgotten about my duffle bag.'

Linc chuckled. 'I guess you're an illegal immigrant, but I think I can trust you. I'm not going to make you bunk down in the airport. You'll be under the watch of the island constabulary, so it's fine. It's too late to get your details over to Brisbane now.' His hand was on my arm and little tingles were firing along the nerve endings.

And not only in my arm.

What was wrong with me?

'I'm sorry. I really have messed up your day, haven't I?' I said.

'Not at all. You've improved it out of sight, and you've solved my problem. And the best part is that David has seen you here with me. That should be the end of this craziness from him. I'll introduce you, and then once he goes back to the Big Island, you can enjoy your holiday in peace.' He flicked a glance back to the customs desk. 'Unless you've changed your mind now that your ex is here? Or about pretending to be my fiancée?'

'No, of course not. And I don't go back on my word.'

'After we've had a drink with David, I'll take you to the Magellan Hotel and I'll make sure you can get into the room you booked.'

'The hotel?' I shook my head. 'I'm not booked into the hotel.'

He frowned. 'There's only one.'

'I'm booked onto a yacht, but I guess with this delay it's going to be too late to get onto it tonight.'

'Which company?

'Luxury Charter Yachts. I've booked a Fusion 40

called *Amore*.'

'What? That's you?' His eyes bored into mine.

'What do you mean that's me?'

'I thought the guest who was coming onto *Amore* was arriving Monday.'

'Duh,' I said. 'Today is Monday. And what does it have to do with you?'

Linc looked uncomfortable. 'Um. The company, that is, Luxury Charter Yachts don't own the fleet. They manage privately owned boats.'

'And?'

We'd reached the luggage carousel and my royal blue duffel bag was completing another circuit of its lonely journey. All the other bags had been claimed.

'Yours?' Linc asked as he reached for it.

'Yes, thank you.' I held my hand out for it, but he shook his head.

'I'll carry it for you.'

'Okay. Now tell me the rest about the yacht.'

'It's a huge coincidence but *Amore* is mine.'

'What?' I stared at him with my mouth open.

'Yes, and I'm pleased we sorted this out before we joined David. Look he's waving to us. If it's mentioned, just say you're staying on my boat.'

'Where do you live?' I asked.

'Don't worry. Not on the boat. I live in the police

residence. I bought *Amore* as an investment instead of a house. Hiring her out is quite lucrative.' He frowned. 'Now I feel guilty that you're paying to be onboard.'

'Don't be silly. You didn't even know me three hours ago.'

'I guess.' He looked around. 'Weren't there two people booked on the charter? Brad?'

I pulled a face. 'It was supposed to be a surprise honeymoon for him after our wedding, and I decided to come by myself.'

'Alone? Do you sail?'

'Yes, alone. And yes, I sail. That's my job. I'm a sailing instructor. Or I was until I quit my job a couple of weeks ago.'

'So, you were planning on sailing around the islands by yourself?'

'Yes, and I'm looking forward to it.'

'Excellent. She's a beautiful boat and one day—sooner rather than later, I hope—I'm going to live on her and sail off into the wide blue yonder.'

I smiled as Linc's words echoed my earlier thoughts.

I was beginning to like the police chief of Deception Island. A lot.

'Come on, David's looking at his watch, and he's one person not to be kept waiting.'

On our way over to the bar, Linc paused at the Customs

desk. 'It's okay, Jen. I'll sort out Jane's paperwork. We've had the royal summons.' He gestured to the president holding court in the bar.

I followed him across to the table feeling as though I was in a movie.

Chapter Seven

Jane

'David, this is Jane. Johnny, I know you've heard lots about her, but you haven't met yet, have you?' Linc's voice was open and friendly, and his mate seemed to pick up on the warning hidden beneath the words. After all, he'd been the one on the other side of the conversation I'd overheard this afternoon.

Linc held the chair while I sat down at the table, and then he sat beside me. He immediately reached over and took my hand, and the president beamed.

'Hello, Jane. It's an absolute pleasure to welcome you to our islands,' the plump older man said. He passed us each a glass of champagne. I felt like chugging it down, but I refrained.

'It's wonderful to be here finally,' I replied with a smile. This was getting easier. I was almost believing the story myself.

And it *was* wonderful to be here. Even with the loss of my passport and money, I was enjoying myself. The only fly in the ointment was the arrival of Brad and Serena. I still couldn't figure out why they were here, but I had no doubt I would find out. They'd seemed as shocked to see me as I had been to see them. But you know what? I didn't even care that they were here. I'd be off on *Amore* and they would hopefully be gone before my charter was over.

I shook my head. How amazing that the yacht belonged to Linc.

'How wonderful you are going to marry our police chief and move to our island,' the president's loud voice interrupted my musing.

I swallowed and nodded. 'Yes. Eventually.'

'Not too long I hope.' His smile was crafty.

This time I shook my head, and Linc chimed in.

'As soon as I can convince her to name the day, David.'

'Well, well, well.' The president rubbed his large hands together. 'I will send a car for you tomorrow, Jane. I'm not going home to Columbus Island until late tomorrow. It will be my pleasure to show you around our beautiful island.'

'Oh, thank you, but I won't be here,' I said before I thought.

Linc's knee pressed against mine and he squeezed my hand beneath the table. 'Jane is a wonderful sailor, and she's taking my yacht out tomorrow.'

The president looked horrified. 'What? Not by herself?'

A ha, I thought. So, I'm supposed to be the little

woman. I might as well have not been there as they spoke.

'Jane is a sailing instructor and I have no hesitation in letting her take my boat out.'

'I thought it was on a honeymoon charter this week,' Johnny said curiously. Linc shot him another warning glance.

Really! Did everyone know everyone's business on this island.

'I cancelled it when I knew Jane was arriving,' Linc said quickly.

'I hope that doesn't lose you too much money, darling,' I said sweetly, and Johnny almost choked on his drink.

'Oh, no. It's just wonderful to have you here, sweetheart.'

'That will absolutely not do.' David put his glass on the table with a thump. 'What were you thinking of, Lincoln?'

'What do you mean, David?' I couldn't help myself.

'Lincoln has a great deal of holiday leave that he never takes. I wonder how he ever found time to spend with you actually.' As the president looked at us over the top of his glasses, it was Linc's turn to choke and cough. Johnny thumped his back.

'How long are you staying, Jane?' David asked.

'Ten days,' I said.

'Then Lincoln, as of this minute you are on ten days recreational leave. I will not let your fiancée sail alone around our islands.'

'Oh no, it's fine. I'll come back every night to see Linc,' I protested.

But the president folded his arms and would not budge. 'Lincoln is now on leave. I know how much he loves to sail. I would not deprive him of your company. My nephew, Thomas will take over the chief of police job until you return in ten days.' He drained his glass, stood and gestured to the two men—obviously minders— sitting at the table beside us. 'It was a pleasure to meet you, Jane. I will look forward to my wedding invitation.'

Linc leaned back with a sigh as soon as the three men exited the terminal. 'Johnny, do me a favour and grab me a beer. I need one.'

His mate grinned at him. 'What did my old gran used to say? "Oh, what a tangled web," and all that.'

'Put a sock in it, pal.'

I looked from one to the other. 'So, what now?'

Johnny looked away and got up and headed for the bar.

Linc sighed. 'We do as we are told.'

'Now hang on one minute. I've paid top dollar to hire your boat. And you—' I poked my finger in his chest '—weren't part of the package.'

'Sorry, Jane. I am now,' he said glumly.

'No.' I folded my arms. I'd learned a lot about being strong over the past few days.

'I don't think you're in a bargaining position.'

'What's that supposed to mean?' I stared at him and got cross with myself when my eyes lingered on his eyes and dark lashes. I dropped my gaze and then they focused on a broad chest with a glimpse of dark chest hair in the V of his shirt.

Would it be so bad to have a sailing partner?

'It means I've let you stay in the country. No passport. No money. No ID. I could deport you.'

'And you'll hold that over me?'

He nodded. 'If it means keeping my job, and not having a wife arranged for me. In a word yes.'

Chapter Eight

Jane

Twenty-four hours later I knew I was in trouble.

Big trouble.

Linc and I had headed to the marina from the airport and we'd boarded *Amore* just after dark. But it was still light enough for me to see that the vessel was every bit as luxurious as the brochure had promised.

Linc preceded me down to the bottom deck and threw my duffel bag into the master cabin. 'You get the good cabin seeing as you're the paying customer.' He'd been snarky ever since we'd left the airport and had stayed that way.

I'd poked about inside and even I'd been impressed by the luxury gold fittings in the large bathroom, and the full-size wardrobe along one side of the cabin. It seemed a shame to throw four pairs of shorts and six T-shirts in there. It looked like it deserved a couple of glam evening dresses.

I tested the bed and smiled; it was feather soft.

When I went back up to the galley, Linc was perusing the contents of the refrigerator. 'You ordered all this?' he said. 'For yourself?'

'I thought there was going to be two of us,' I defended

myself.

He pulled out a bottle of Moet and then pointed at the two lobster salads sitting on the shelf. 'It's a waste not to eat it.'

'Are you going to keep that scowl for ten days?' I said. 'It will play havoc with your digestion.'

'I'm sorry. It's been one hell of a day.' Finally, he grinned and, I won't say my insides melted, but it sure felt like they did.

Big trouble.

Not the fact that I had no money, and no passport, but the fact that every time this man looked at me, or spoke to me, my hormones went 'oh yeah', without my permission.

We went to bed early—in separate cabins—after polishing off the bottle of champagne and the delectable salad, not to mention the two slices of chocolate cheesecake that were in the fridge.

'Do you want to take her out?' Linc asked after I wandered up in a pair of shorts and a singlet top, early the next morning.

'I'd love to.' I'd pored over the charts for the past two weeks, and I'd already logged a charter route with the Charter Yacht company. That had been the hard part; there were so many islands to explore. 'You trust me?'

He nodded. 'I've checked you out online. You've got some sailing awards behind you. I was impressed.'

I couldn't help the blush that warmed my cheeks.

'I've got some calls to make before we lose phone range. And a passport to chase up.'

'I thought you were off duty now. But thank you.'

The only downside of the morning was the sight of Brad and Serena walking along the path at the edge of the marina as we'd prepared to leave. I couldn't help the little surge of glee when I saw the angry expression on Brad's face, and the way Serena walked behind him. I made sure they didn't see me. Eventually they headed around the point and out of sight.

I went down to the cabin and picked up my phone. At least I had that.

I dialled home and braced myself. 'Hi, Mum. It's me,' I said when my mother answered.

'Jane. Where are you? We've been beside ourselves. Poor Brad is almost suicidal.'

I snorted. 'Is he? Where is he?'

'Joanie is distraught. She said he was so devastated by what you'd done and the embarrassment of being left at the altar, he's gone off to an island to recover. I don't think she'll ever forgive you. She's worried about his mental health.'

'Which island?'

'Oh, I don't know. She said he's gone to some small island where no one will know him. He got a standby flight and it was cheap. He spent all his investment savings on that beautiful house he bought for you. That's why he went to this island. It was all he could afford.'

'And all my savings,' I muttered

'What? What did you say? Speak up Jane. Don't mumble.'

'I said, by himself. Did he go by himself?'

'Of course, he's by himself. The poor boy is heartbroken. Joanie wanted to go with him, but he said he'd preferred to be alone to get over it. Are you thinking of going looking for him? Where are you anyway?'

No "we've been worried about you, dear daughter". In that instant I decided I would do anything I could to get a sailing job out here on one of the islands.

'I just wanted to let you know I'm sailing and I'm fine, in case you were worried.'

Silence, so obviously not.

'Okay, Mum. Just thought I'd touch base. Bye.' I pressed END before she could argue.

I made my way back up to the deck, and my mouth dried as I spotted Linc at the front of the boat with his phone to his ear.

Bare-chested and in a pair of board shorts.

Chapter Nine

Linc

The phone call to Brisbane Airport was quick and had an excellent outcome. Efficient Andre had been waiting for Linc's call, and he'd organised for Jane's folder, passport and money to be sent securely on the first flight to the islands this morning. Linc called Johnny and filled him in, and he promised to collect them, and give them to Jennifer to lock in the safe at the airport terminal.

Movement in the galley caught his attention, and a minute later Jane appeared on the deck. He groaned; the first sight of her in those shorts and the skimpy singlet top had almost done his head in. The second glimpse got a reaction from the rest of him.

God, she was drop dead gorgeous. Even though she was not very slim, she was in good shape, and he could see the whipcord tautness in her muscles as she walked across the deck to him.

'Are you right to get underway?' he asked gruffly. His head was so full of Jane he'd forgotten about her passport and stuff already.

'Sure am. Who's the skipper? You, the owner, or me,

the client?' Her grin was cheeky.

'It's your charter, so you tell me where we're heading today.'

'I found a nice little mooring on the map on one of the southern islands. It's called Crystal Cove. I'd planned it for my first night. Do you know it?'

'Do I know it? I grew up in these islands. I've been sailing since I could walk.'

'Really?'

'Well, maybe I was a bit older.' Linc walked back to the helm near the door to the saloon. 'I'll get the engines going and turn us into the wind. You unlace the sail bag and get the main up.' He focused most of his attention on the channel out of the marina as Jane did as he'd instructed.

Most of his attention, anyway. It was hard not to admire the muscles working in her arms and calves as she pulled the halyard and the mainsail unfurled.

He had no doubt Jane knew what she was doing by the time they were underway. She took over the helm as the wind pushed them south and he smiled as she admired the small islands they sailed past.

'It's beautiful,' she called to him.

'And so are you,' he thought.

'How about a coffee for the skipper?' Her grin was wide as the wind caught her loose hair and whipped it around her face.

'Aye, aye captain.' He returned the grin and headed down to the galley.

***

I was aware that Linc was watching me, and I can't say that I didn't enjoy it. It had been a while since anyone had looked at me with admiration. As he handed me my coffee, our fingers brushed, and he pulled his hand away so quickly I almost dropped the mug.

We reached Crystal Cove by lunchtime, and I was so taken with it, I could have spent the whole ten days there. It was one of those perfect coral islands that you see on the tourist brochures. Pure white sand, palm trees waving in the breeze, and translucent blue water. This was Mother Nature at her best. No photoshopped colours.

Paradise.

'What's the plan, captain?' Linc asked as we headed down to the galley once we were moored.

'Swim, sleep, read, eat.'

'In that order?' he joked. 'I'm starving.'

'Okay. Eat first. Then sleep, swim, read, sleep. How does that sound?'

The galley was small, and it was hard to prepare lunch without brushing against each other constantly.

Although the fourth time Linc reached past me and his arm brushed the side of my left breast, I wondered if it was deliberate. My awareness of him was so strong, it was a wonder he didn't run a mile.

Eventually we'd prepared sandwiches and a cheese platter, and as I went to head up to the deck, Linc pointed to the fridge. 'A drink?'

'Hmm. Maybe. What are you having?'

'A beer,' he replied.

'Okay. I'll have a wine. Thanks.'

I carried the tray with the food, and he came behind me with the drinks. We settled on the comfortable lounges behind the helm.

'I forgot to tell you that I had success with our friend, Andre this morning.'

'Yes?' I paused as I reached for a sandwich.

'Success. You're no longer an illegal immigrant.' He glanced down at his watch. 'Your passport should just about be locked in the safe at our airport now. Along with your money and your folder.'

'Oh, thank you.' I put my hand on my chest and his gaze followed it down there. A shivery warmth ran down my spine, and I realised I'd never felt like this with Brad.

With anyone.

'That's a huge relief.'

'My pleasure.'

We spent the afternoon frolicking in the water and walking along the beach collecting shells. *Amore* was the only boat in the bay and this paradise was ours alone.

We swam back to the yacht and Linc pulled himself up the ladder before holding his hand out to me.

His grip was strong, and his hand warm despite being wet. He pulled me aboard and I stumbled as I stepped off the ladder. His arms opened and I fell against him. Linc's chest was hard and warm and bare against my skin.

His groan echoed the way I was feeling. His arms went around me holding me close.

'Do you mind if I get something out of the way, and then this tension that's between us might go away?'

'What would that something be?' My voice was husky.

His hands lifted and his fingers were gentle as he slowly pushed my wet hair from my face. Almost reverently Linc cupped my cheeks in his hands while his eyes stayed on mine. Slowly . . . oh, so slowly . . . he lowered his head until we were a breath apart. He closed his eyes and those gorgeous eyelashes caressed my cheeks when he opened his eyes again.

I drew a sharp breath as his lips brushed my closed eyelids. No one had ever kissed me like this before. His lips slid down my cheek until his mouth hovered above mine.

I opened my eyes and the look that passed between us was electric as he caught my bottom lip between his.

I sighed against his mouth and I was lost.

***

Ten days later.

It's hard to believe that one kiss can be life changing, but that first kiss Linc and I shared in the airport on that first day in paradise might have happened too soon—after all he first kissed me less than twenty-four hours after I'd overheard that conversation about my "fat arse"—but it was a kiss that I believe was destined to change my life.

Love at first sight.

I chuckled as I rolled over in the bed where Linc had left me to go and check the anchor. He had been a gentleman and I had spent the first two nights alone in the master cabin, before I'd enticed him in on our third night at Crystal Cove. Our days—and now our nights—had been perfection in this pristine lagoon, and we saw no reason to move on. We had one more night left in our paradise.

Linc had radioed the base, so the charter company knew where we were.

I climbed out of bed and took a quick shower—fresh water was scarce unless we went somewhere to top up—and I had been more than content to spend our ten days here.

Linc was leaning over the bow and I went over and stood beside him. 'Problem?'

'No, all good.' He pulled me close and kissed me before he continued. 'But it's just as well I got up because I think we might move on today. We've got company.' He pointed over my shoulder and I turned in his arms. A charter boat loaded with tourists was coming into the bay.

Our bay.

'Oh no. I guess being in paradise couldn't last forever.'

His arms stayed around me and Linc lowered his forehead to touch mine.

'Depends what you mean by paradise.'

'What do you mean?'

'How would you feel about staying in the islands?'

'Why?' I asked slowly. 'So David doesn't hassle you about a wife?'

'No. It has nothing to do with David.' His eyes held mine and a tremor went through me. 'Do you believe in love at first sight, Jane?'

'Will I be honest?'

'Yes, please.' Linc's lips were close, and his breath was warm against mine.

'I didn't. In fact, I had no idea what love was until . . .'

'Until?' His lips were a whisper from mine. I was barely aware of the whistles coming from the boat as it motored past and *Amore* rocked in its wake.

'Until you kissed me the other day.'

'And I didn't believe in love at first sight, until a beautiful little spitfire bailed me up in a plane, and I looked into a gorgeous pair of green eyes. I was lost from that moment, Jane.'

Certainty that Linc was the man of my dreams built as I smiled up at him.

'Will you stay in the islands, so we can explore what we have and see where it takes us?' Linc's forehead rested on mime.

'I'll have to get a job and find somewhere to live.'

'We can sort all that. And weekends when I'm not working, we can explore on *Amore*. What do you think?'

'I think it is very fitting that your boat is called *Amore* and . . .'

The rest of my answer was made with my lips against Linc's.

Epilogue

A light breeze drifted across the sand as the guests assembled on the beach at Crystal Cove. Three rows of chairs sat near the water on the edge of the pure white sand. Linc and his best man, Johnny, stood next to the celebrant, and much to Jane's mother's displeasure, Linc wore a pair of white board shorts and a Hawaiian shirt.

Her mother and father sat in the front row on one side of the semi-circle, and on the other side was the president, his wife, and his two ever-present minders. Linc's parents were sailing in the Mediterranean and they had Skyped them last night.

David winked at Linc and gave him a thumbs up. 'You've made an excellent choice, Lincoln. I couldn't have picked a better wife for you.'

In the second and third row was the small group of sailing friends they had made over the past twelve months, as Jane had worked at the sailing school, and between lessons had moonlighted as a sailing guide with Luxury Charter Yachts.

The sound of a boat's motor vied with the swishing of the waves on the beach. A small rubber tender appeared around the point and Linc's heart swelled as he saw Jane's hair blowing in the breeze.

He smiled as she stepped barefooted from the small boat onto the sand. Her white dress was simple, and she had laced white flowers through her hair.

David stood and his clear pure voice filled the air as he sang an island wedding greeting.

Jane stepped over to Linc, and she blinked tears away as David's voice faded.

'That greeting was so beautiful,' she whispered.

'Not as beautiful as you are, my love.'

A breeze light as a baby's breath and as warm as a kiss, surrounded them with the fragrance of the tropics as they promised their lives to each other.

When the celebrant told Linc to kiss his bride, he held her at arm's length and held her eyes with his.

'No kiss will ever compare with the first kiss we shared out in that bay.'

'It will,' she whispered. 'Our first kiss as husband and wife.

And Jane Martin proceeded to show her new husband exactly that.

THE END

A special thank you to my wonderful editor and critique partner, Susanne Bellamy, and my eagle-eyed proof-reader, Kristen Woolgar.

Short and Sweet: 2

Second Chance Cafe

Susanne Bellamy

Dedication:

For Anna, who shared our lives for twelve wonderful years. May there be a never-ending supply of bones and cheese, and hugs galore, beautiful girl.

Chapter One

Julie Aster sat in the middle of Queen's Park off-leash area and leaned back on her elbows. The park was a sea of shimmering greens, glowing under the early summer sun. Turning her face towards its mid-morning warmth, she closed her eyes and let her thoughts drift. Sending the last box of lying Travis' abandoned gear to charity closed a chapter in her life, one that her friends encouraged her to put behind her as quickly as possible. Betrayal hurt—big time—but she'd learned her lesson. She wasn't about to forget it; not when so many lives depended on her.

Her hand reached out to pat Anna, and met empty air. Her German Shepherd never left her side without permission. Unease slithered through her mind like the beginning of a stress headache and Heaven knew she'd had enough of those in the last couple of months. Sitting up, she scanned the immediate area.

Cupping her hands around her mouth, she called,

"Anna." *Where have you got to, girl?*

Champion novice dog at puppy training school, Anna simply did not wander far from her mistress. Flutters of concern stirred in Julie's belly and she put her fingers to her mouth and whistled. Piercing and loud, the whistle cut through the joyful shouts of a group of youngsters playing footy on the neighbouring oval.

Movement off to the side caught her eye and two streaks, one golden and the other, black, raced out of dense shade at the edge of the off-leash area, scattering a flock of wood pigeons. Not one but two dogs raced towards her.

A huge black Shepherd, the biggest Julie had seen, followed Anna across the lush green grass. Anna came straight to her and sat on her left, smiling to show she was very pleased with her discovery, or so Julie interpreted her doggie grin. The black dog dropped beside Anna. A metal, bone-shaped identity tag hung from his collar and caught the light as he turned his head towards her.

"Found a friend, did you? Where's your owner, boy?" Julie presented her closed hand for the dog to smell then hunkered down to pat both Anna and her new friend. "He's a handsome fellow, isn't he, Anna? Seems like this park is doggie-dating heaven."

A shadow fell across them and a deep voice rumbled above their heads. "Bear's been making friends, I see, and with the best-looking females in the city."

Tingles of awareness ran down Julie's spine at the sound of the whisky-smooth voice. Her imagination went into overdrive, creating an image of a man to match such a voice.

Silly, you know you'll be disappointed.

Wanting to hold onto the image a moment longer, she fiddled with Anna's collar and patted her dog's blonde head. Anna's gentle chocolate-brown eyes looked up into Anna's, and a pink tongue flicked her nose as she waited, body quivering with anticipation.

"Bear? Suits him." Steeling herself against inevitable disappointment, her gaze lifted, following the line of a pair of denim-clad legs and Jimmy Barnes T-shirt that showed off a toned and muscled torso, and up to the face of Bear's owner. Stubbled cheeks, and with light brown hair pulled back into a stubby ponytail, his smile was warm and open. Cinnamon-brown eyes crinkled at the corners.

Belly flutters that had subsided with Anna's reappearance returned as full-sized butterflies swarming around their favourite plants. Ruggedly handsome in an outdoorsy way, Bear's owner had a killer smile, *and* a German Shepherd. And despite the cheesy pick-up line, entries two and three on Julie's wish list—her *pre-Travis* wish list—stood before her rolled into one very tall . . . and attractive package.

Add the sexy voice and she was probably drooling as much as Anna.

Julie's hand tightened on Anna's collar as she struggled to come up with a witty comment. Her mouth opened and closed while Bear's owner hunkered down and wrapped an arm over his dog and stroked Anna's head.

"Your dog is lovely. No wonder Bear was— interested." His eyebrow rose cheekily as he stood and held out one hand. "Jack Schultz."

She reached over Anna and shook his hand, surprised to find him towering above her. At five-feet-nine, she often looked guys directly in the eye. "I'm Julie Aster and this is Anna."

"So, Julie and Anna Aster, can Bear and I interest you in a coffee? I spotted a van somewhere around here yesterday."

Julie checked her watch. Currently, the coffee

cart was manned by one of her volunteer staff and her shift didn't start for another thirty minutes. "Thanks. That'd be nice. You're new to town?" Keeping Anna at heel, Julie strolled beside Jack and Bear towards the brightly painted 'Coffee to go' sign.

"Yes, just arrived. I'm running the Millhouse Tavern until it sells." They joined the short line of customers and Bear sat, head turned to Anna. Tongues hanging out, both dogs appeared to be smiling at each other.

Saturday in the park on a glorious summer day was bright with promise. For both of them. Anna had to like any guy Julie brought home and Jack and Bear had been an instant hit if the canine equivalent of sparks zapping between the dogs was any indication.

Another tick on my wish list. At this rate, I'll have our wedding and honeymoon arranged before we finish coffee.

Travis. Don't forget what he did to you. The snarky voice in her head wiped the smile off her face and she realised Jack was waiting for her to speak.

"Um . . . I thought the Millhouse owner went bankrupt? I mean—" Jack watched her through half-closed eyes and she bent to fold Anna's lead under her collar. "Sorry. I didn't mean to pry."

"The owner is in financial difficulty but I've come in to keep the pub going and try to improve its saleability, that sort of thing."

"So, are you a receiver?"

"Yeah." The customers ahead of them moved off with their takeaways and he stepped up to the fold-up table that was their service counter.

Marsha, a senior high school student who volunteered every weekend, greeted them. "Hi, Julie. What can I get for you?" The teenager looked at Julie but her gaze kept flicking to Jack.

"The usual, thanks. Anna too. Ah, Jack, what would you like?"

"Espresso shot and Bear will have what Anna's having."

"Right away, sir." Marsha's gaze was pinned on Jack as she backed into Doug, another of the shelter's volunteers who Julie had high hopes of training up to take on more responsibility.

Coffee slopped over Doug's hand. "Hey, Marsha, babe, watch what you're doing." Doug flicked coffee off his hand and swiped a couple of drops from his shirt.

"Sorry, Doug." Pink-cheeked, Marsha bit her lip and turned away to fill their order.

Marsha's clumsiness drew the attention of three female customers in the line before the women looked back to Jack. The new arrival was sending out pheromones by the bucketful.

Julie covered a smile and reached down to stroke Anna. "Bear will love our doggie biscuits. We bake special nutritious treats each week and—"

"We? Do you work here too?"

"The coffee cart brings us extra funds, but I manage the centre and the adoption process when we make a match for our rescue animals."

He grinned and laughter lines crinkled around his eyes. "A match as in what? A dating service for canines?"

Laughter bubbled up and burst from her lips. A sense of humour rated high and Jack had just scored another tick on her wish list. The way her libido was dancing, make that two ticks. His smile was worth an extra tick all on its own.

Whoa, girl. Remember Travis.

"Every few months we have a sort of pet parade and find new owners for as many of our rescue animals as we can."

"Like those art shows where you ply patrons with plenty of bubbly and get them to part with megabucks?"

"We put on coffee and biscuits before the parade but no bubbly. Responsible pet ownership is important, especially for pets that have been dumped. Full information about each animal is given and we offer short counselling sessions about the care and commitment needed to take on a pet. It's for life—at least, for the life of the pet." Julie groaned softly. She'd just morphed into teacher mode and lectured the hottest guy she'd met since . . . forever.

Heat scorched her cheeks. Unable to meet the glazed expression she was sure he would be wearing, she reached down and patted Anna. "Sorry, I get carried away at times."

"You're passionate about what you do. Don't ever apologise for that."

She looked up. Jack's eyes weren't glazed over in boredom but bright with approval. Warmth zinged through her body until she was sure she would self-combust. Interest rarely met her lessons on responsible pet ownership, and Jack's was special, not solely because appreciation rarely came her way.

"Thanks. It's great when one of our animals finds a new home."

"And the ones you can't find a match for?"

Julie's smile slipped away. The worst part of rescuing pets was knowing some of them would never find another home. "They're euthanised after a period of waiting. The coffee van supplements the shortfall in government funding, but you'd be surprised how high costs can run. I just wish—"

"It's not possible to save every one of them." Understanding shaded his response and sympathy shone from his eyes.

"No. It's not."

Marsha placed their takeaway cups on the counter and added a plastic bowl containing six bone-shaped biscuits.

Jack glanced at her name badge with a smile. "Thanks, Marsha."

Marsha met his gaze briefly then, with cheeks that grew pinker with each passing second, she muttered, "Enjoy your coffees," and moved on to the next customer.

Jack stacked the cups and lifted both in one hand while Julie collected the doggie treats. She followed him to a low brick wall that offered seating in front of the derelict park café. Abandoned, she'd considered tendering for it when she'd begun at the centre. Running the animal shelter was a tightrope operation and gambling their small surplus on a risky venture—like her ex-boyfriend, Travis had done—wasn't in her nature. Lies and more lies to cover up his losses had nearly brought her undone. She had trusted Travis, foolishly agreeing to a joint bank account, and he'd betrayed that trust.

Worse than that had been how close the shelter had come to closing because Travis had ripped off a chunk of the operating funds.

The dogs dropped in front of their humans, noses almost touching.

Jack picked up one of the dog treats and traced the stamped comment in the biscuit. "'I love my dog.' Cute." He offered the biscuit and Bear took it gently.

Julie gave Anna a biscuit. Stereo crunching floated up before Julie turned her attention back to Jack. "We cook several healthy treats but these are Anna's favourites. Looks like they're a hit with Bear, too."

"I must get some to take home with me."

"Oh, we don't have a takeaway option."

Jack tilted his head and pinned her with a searching gaze. "Why not? It would be a great money-spinner. Pre-packaged single item or combos. Haven't customers asked for them yet?"

"Well—yes. But all our staff are volunteers. We'd have to take on a paid part-time cook and set up a kitchen to achieve that, and I doubt we can afford to."

"Ever heard the saying, *to make money, you have to spend some*? Let me put it another way, if I could show you there's a market for homemade, takeaway dog treats, would you reconsider?" He watched her with an intensity that would usually have made her uncomfortable. Only this time, her brain whirled with possibilities. How many pets could they save if they had more funds?

Jack stood and offered a hand. Without thinking, she took it. He pulled her to her feet and headed for a tree where three older ladies sat chatting while their pets socialised at their feet. As one, the women looked up and checked out the six feet plus of delectable male heading their way.

"Good morning, ladies, lovely day, isn't it.

We're conducting a little informal survey and wondered if you have a moment to help us out?"

"Sure, hon. What can we help you with?"

"I see your dogs are enjoying some of the coffee cart treats. Would you be interested in purchasing a regular weekly supply if they were available?"

A grey-haired woman who appeared to be the oldest of the three piped up. "I'd put in a standing order. Archie loves his oaties but it's a long wait for him between visits. At his age, he should be enjoying them every day."

"Thanks."

Her companions agreed, as did most of the other dog owners they surveyed. Flutters of excitement filled Julie as she and Jack walked back to their brick perch. Their knees bumped as he sat facing her, and heat trickled through her body. Beneath his charming cinnamon gaze, she read an answering awareness before he turned away.

He began coiling and uncoiling Bear's lead. "I reckon there's untapped potential in your coffee cart idea. With proper advertising, takeaway treats could add to your coffers and that's just for a start. I've several other ideas if you'd care to hear them. What do you think?"

Bemused by the unusual turn her morning had taken, Julie shook her head. "You're like the answer to my prayer. Where did you come from?"

"Camooweal via Longreach," he deadpanned, and then winked. It was the wink that won her.

"Is this the sort of thing you do when you *rescue* businesses?"

"Sometimes. Not that yours is in need of rescue. It looks like it's doing well."

"But if we can do better—"

"You can save more animals."

"I'll run the costs past my accountant." Anything that would save animals' lives had to be considered. And gorgeous Jack was like her personal knight in shining armour.

"I can run some numbers for you—if you like?" The light in his eyes suddenly dimmed as though shutters closed and he turned away.

His momentary hesitation brought her down to earth with a jolt. Who in their right mind would open their finances to a stranger? She'd only just met this guy. Seemed the thought had occurred to Jack as well.

"Sorry, I didn't mean to poke my nose into your

business. Take it to your accountant." He reached down to stroke Bear's head, and their easy banter dried up. He tossed back his espresso and stood. Bear rose and looked up expectantly. "I only meant to give Bear a quick walk before I opened the pub. Better be on my way. I enjoyed meeting you, Julie and Anna Aster."

"Jack, I— me, too."

"See you around." He strode off, Bear by his side.

As Jack left, Marsha approached and plopped down beside Julie.

"Is it my shift already?"

"Yeah. Any idea how long the hottie is staying in town?"

The hottie. Jack's that all right. Every female in the area had cast covetous glances her way but she had claimed his full attention. *Anna and me.*

"Probably not long."

Marsha turned on her phone. "Pity."

And that thought depressed her too. He was here for the short-term only, until the tavern was back on solid ground. His work would take him away to—to blasted Camooweal or the back of beyond. And that was just as well given her good intentions not to forget the lessons learned from Travis' betrayal seemed to have blown away on the summer breeze.

But if I had a dollar for every item Jack ticked off my list, I'd keep the centre open for a year!

"Yes, it is a pity." Julie headed over to the coffee cart to begin her shift. She set Anna's water bowl out behind the cart, pulled on a fresh apron and then cleaned her hands with sanitiser. Scanning the crowds, her attention snagged on the distant figures of Jack and Bear before they turned and were lost to sight.

Pity.

If Jack Schultz was as honest as he was good-looking, he ticked her wish list boxes with neon-bright, bold ticks.

Blast that list, and blast Travis for taking her optimism and trust and twisting it into something dark and shrivelled. Jack Shultz seemed decent and charming, but she wasn't about to let him close. Her heart was under lock and key. Once burned, twice shy and all that. If Jack had ideas that could increase profits and offer future stability for the shelter, great. But nothing and no one would put the shelter in danger again.

Including her.

Chapter Two

Jack wiped down the bar and lifted the stools ready for the cleaners in the morning. He switched off the main lights, flicked on the alarm and locked the door. "Come on, Bear, let's go get some fresh air."

Bear trotted by his side through the midnight-quiet streets. Mist hung between the trees and twigs rolled underfoot as they retraced their morning route through the park. Ahead of them, the empty café appeared to float, insubstantial as a dream on a layer of white-grey cloud. Detached from the everyday world, it precisely suited Jack's mood.

He sat on the brick wall between concrete and grass, and mulled over his meeting with Julie. Her excitement at his suggestion had led to him almost giving himself away, blurting out that he'd run the numbers for her.

Typical accountant reaction.

The tavern was his escape; his excuse to get away from the family business and his overbearing father while he considered his plans, not to make life more complicated by involving himself in a pet rescue operation—or getting entangled with the local lovelies. But helping Julie was the right thing to do.

Mist coalesced into Julie's heart-shaped face and cornflower-blue eyes, before an errant breeze dispersed the cloudy image.

Jack rubbed Bear's ears. "You're to blame, old fella. If you hadn't chased Anna, I wouldn't have met her mistress."

And that meeting could complicate his plans. His stomach clenched and he drew a deep breath. Why couldn't his parents understand his need to explore other alternatives to the family business? A pub with potential but suffering from poor management had given him scope to be creative. And time to think about what he wanted.

Shadowy tree trunks loomed ghostly in the misty light. Jack snorted. "More tree change than sea change, hey, Bear?" No matter how appealing the distraction, a romantic involvement was the last thing he needed until he knew where he wanted to be. There was enough pressure from his parents on that front. His most recent discussion with his parents replayed on an endless loop in his brain.

'Accountants make good, steady money, son. It's a safe job and you can stay close to home.' Of course his mother wanted him close by. Grandchildren were dear to her heart and, since his older sister had moved to Adelaide, maternal pressure to get married had increased. Which was why he'd used the receiver's job in this inland city as an escape, even for a few weeks.

Already, he'd put plans in place to refurbish the outdoor area and renovations of the main bar had begun. But how much longer would it occupy him? It was, after all, an easy fix. Julie's concerns about her animals were more difficult.

'And the ones you can't match?'

He could have kicked himself for asking such an insensitive question. Given her distress over losing any animal, he suspected she had a soft heart.

He understood that sort of love. If anything happened to Bear, he'd be devastated. But he wasn't in town to solve other people's problems. Not that Julie had a problem. She hadn't even asked for his help so why was his mind dwelling on her?

He rubbed Bear's velvety ears. "Hey, Bear, we'll just have to forego the pleasure of their company and take our walks early and late. Besides, I should be focused on setting the pub up for re-sale, not trying for creative solutions to a problem that's not mine."

***

The sun played hide and seek between the trunks of camphor laurels as Julie jogged with Anna by her side. A few runners and a couple of walkers smiled in passing, but this early on a Sunday they mostly had the paths to themselves.

Two circuits later Julie headed for her stretching spot by the disused café. She unclipped Anna's leash and hung it over the brick wall and then placed her foot beside the strip of pink leather and reached for her toes. Ants scurried in a busy line and leaves swirled at her feet as she sifted through her meeting with Jack and Bear. *Again*.

Ideas about a takeaway service had skittered through her brain and kept her awake past midnight. But Jack's abrupt departure left her with unanswered questions and a burning desire to learn more.

Anna whined and yipped, the short sound her doggie version of welcome. Next moment, Bear's moist black nose pressed against Julie's leg and a pair of fluorescent orange running shoes appeared in her peripheral vision. Bear whined in greeting.

Jack was standing beside them, hands on hips and breathing hard.

Conscious of her dishevelment and sweaty body, Julie dropped her leg and faced him, hoping he'd read her red cheeks as a sign of hard work exercising rather than embarrassment. She wiped a sweaty forearm across her cheeks and mouth. "Hi. You're a runner too?"

"Clears my head—usually. Bear led me here. Now I know what had him so interested." Bear and Anna dropped side by side and Jack dropped Bear's lead across the dog's broad back.

"Anna. They want to play." Julie laughed and brushed strands of hair from her forehead as she sat on the wall. She looked up and her pulse spiked.

Jack's running vest left his muscled shoulders and arms mostly bare and clung to his chest, delineating a physique that ticked off yet one more item on her wish list. Anna wasn't the only one who wanted to play.

Julie ran her tongue across salty lips and forced her attention back to his face. "Jack, about yesterday— you mentioned you had more ideas to increase profit for the shelter. Did you mean it?" If his informal survey was indicative of dog-owners' interest, the shelter could be onto a winner.

"Uh, sure. Happy to help." His gaze stayed on her, but subtly, his focus sharpened as he ticked off items on his fingers. "Check with your accountant before you make any firm decisions, but I can give you a reasonable estimate of cost analysis for consideration. Let's start with the dog biscuits. I'll need costs of ingredients, containers, labelling etcetera from you but I can look up the rates for a casual cook. Then there's compliance costs for the kitchen where you make the biscuits, leasing the space, council permits and—"

"Whoa! I thought we were talking about a small operation with few overheads and mostly profit for the shelter. This sounds bigger than *Jurassic Park*."

"Everything needs to be done by the book. You can't move into larger scale production in a home kitchen." Jack frowned and she wondered if she had been naïve in her expectations of how much profit would be made for the shelter.

"Council compliance sounds expensive." The therapeutic effects of her early morning run disappeared as tension pulled her neck muscles tight. For a guy who worked as a receiver, Jack seemed to know a lot about setting up a business kitchen.

"Even with setup costs, I still believe the longer term outlook for success is good. Better than good."

Getting carried away and forgetting to take a reality check had hampered her first attempts at bailing the sinking shelter out of trouble. Travis' theft of her money had compounded the problem. Never again. "I realise long-term prospects have to be factored in, but we can't afford to dip into the red. Not even briefly."

"Once you get the operation up and running there are certain economies of scale, but the initial set up will cost a bit. Look, why don't you pop into the tavern for lunch and we can chat some more about it. Bring whatever figures you can and we'll go from there." Relaxed and gorgeous and so very confident and convincing, Jack crossed his arms over his chest and waited.

What could she say? That she wanted to turn tail and run because he'd offered her what she wanted? Did he honestly believe in the potential of the doggie treats? His certainty bolstered her flagging enthusiasm. Cautious by nature, giving Jack a chance to work through the numbers wasn't a gamble. It was just that, in her head, she'd already spent the extra money without taking account of the expenses.

"My shout. And at least then you'll have more information before you make a decision. Lunch, info, and my company—what more could you want?" He winked, and she allowed his confidence and enthusiasm to take her along for the ride.

"Do you really think it's worth it?"

A hot easterly wind set the leaves overhead madly dancing and his slow smile heated her. "Don't tell me you're giving up before you've begun? Let me show you the bigger picture."

Chapter Three

As Jack pulled another beer, he glanced at the door for the hundredth time since the lunch session had begun. Food service was almost over and the Sunday crowd had settled in front of various wide screens showing sports from golf, to fishing, and motor racing. He handed over a schooner of beer to the waiting patron. "There you go, sport."

She wasn't coming. He should have eased into talking about setup costs once she was here.

Not that it was any skin off his nose if Julie didn't come.

One less task to work on.

But despite his conviction he didn't want or need to complicate his life, there was something about her. Normally he avoided women who wore their heart on their sleeve and Julie was a soft touch where animals were concerned. But she wasn't just some passionate do-gooder. Google had thrown up some interesting details.

It seemed she had rescued the rescue centre from almost certain closure and turned its fortunes around.

Which didn't mean there wasn't more that could be done to secure its future. He had ideas . . . but if she wasn't prepared to take a risk, there was little point dwelling on them.

He turned on the tap and rinsed off a tray of glasses before loading the dishwasher.

A warm wind gusted through the bar as the front door opened and closed and he prepared for the disappointment of it not being her—again.

But there she was . . . walking into the bar. Her long chestnut hair was pulled back into a braid but tendrils framed her face as she stopped and looked around. He raised a wet hand in greeting and grinned. "Thought you were going to stand me up."

She hugged her laptop to her chest. "It took me a while to find the figures you wanted, and then I had to make a spread sheet and—"

"It's fine, Julie. I was teasing."

"Actually, you looked preoccupied. Are you sure this is a good time for you?"

Nervous as the skittish filly he remembered from his childhood riding lessons, she sidestepped towards the door.

Jack ambled around the end of the counter and gently took her elbow and guided her away from the door. "Your timing's perfect. I'm just finishing the lunch shift and I'm starving. Do you like steak sandwiches? We've got a new sauce that—"

She shook her head. "I'm vegetarian. Look, don't worry about lunch. I know the pub's specialty is steak."

"Well now, the chef has revamped our offerings. She's got a mushroom risotto patty with roast pumpkin and onion jam that would make it onto the menu of a fancy restaurant. How's that sound?"

Julie caught her lower lip in her teeth before a grin spread over her face. "Wonderful. Yes, please."

"Great. I kept a table for us where it's a bit quieter." He led her to the corner table with a reserved sign and a view over the newly created railway parkland precinct and held her chair as she sat. "I'll put in our lunch orders and be right back. Drink?"

"Lemon, lime and bitters please. No ice." She set her laptop on the table and crossed her arms on top of it.

"Coming right up."

FOUR SEASONS SHORT AND SWEET

The windowpanes rattled as the summer wind picked up and a table of patrons rose with their drinks in hand and headed inside. Heavy clouds were growing on the eastern horizon, building up to another mid-afternoon summer storm, but Julie was here and sitting at one of his tables. To Jack, the afternoon was just fine.

Julie glanced through the window and pressed her hands to her stomach. Okay, she'd slightly exaggerated the time it had taken her to collate the information Jack had requested. Once he'd left her this morning, caution and jitters had warred in her stomach until she'd all but convinced herself the whole idea was ridiculous and lunch with Jack would be a waste of both their time.

Sunday morning wasn't her rostered day at the rescue centre, but, as often happened when faced with a difficult decision, she'd ended up popping in. One special mother-to-be, Lolly, a *bitsa* with some Labrador in her bloodline, was close to full term. Budget constraints were already tight, and how they were going to find homes for all of Lolly's litter worried Julie. Extra funding and more foster carers would make a huge difference to their survival. Jack seemed confident about the proposed fundraising. But maybe the numbers he had come up with would dash her hopes.

And so she dithered and decided not to keep their appointment.

Until she remembered his smile and that wink.

"Here you go, one LLB, no ice." Jack placed a tall glass on a coaster in front of her and sat in the chair opposite her. He raised his glass of water and drank half of it in one go. "Thirsty work."

"So I see. Don't tell me the pub's got no beer?"

He laughed and sat back, and set his glass down on a coaster. "Plenty on tap but I prefer not to drink when I work. So, busy morning?"

Sitting across the table, the embodiment of her wish list smiled and heavens, if he didn't make her forget her own name. His smile set off flutters in her stomach and she pressed her thighs together. Scrambling for something non-personal, she fell back on work. "I've got a bitsa mum due to whelp soon and little chance of placing her pups if the litter is big, which I think it will be."

"So the pressure's on, hey?"

"We need to either expand our operation or advertise to find new foster homes. Both require more funds than we've got." In fact, the amount she'd calculated they would need was unlikely to come from doggie treat sales.

"Shall we eat first then go over the figures? I've had a couple of other ideas that could help."

##

Julie saved the summary she had created and closed her laptop. "I'm impressed, Jack. We could have the doggie treats underway in no time and the other suggestions—your ideas are creative and cost effective."

Jack grinned and stretched his arms over his head. Today he wore an Eagles T-shirt that pulled out of his low-slung jeans, revealing a flat stomach and a tan he could only have acquired by living at the coast. Was it an all-over tan, all the way down to—?

He lowered his arms and hooked his thumbs into his pockets.

Julie dragged her gaze upwards and met his amused brown eyes. Ogling him was fine; getting caught in the act was plain embarrassing. She cleared her throat. "I'll work on the forms tonight. The sooner they're submitted, the sooner we can begin promotion of phase one."

"I can probably speed up the application process

for the kitchen through council if you're committed to the idea. I know someone—"

"—who knows someone. Yeah, I get how it works." Julie couldn't keep the bitter note out of her voice.

Jack's forehead wrinkled in a slight frown. "You sound like you've had a bad experience? Or don't you like the idea of special consideration?"

"Someone who knew someone put in an objection to the first proposed expansion of the centre. We lost numerous animals that could have been rehoused in the new complex during the delay until our appeal was heard. The objector didn't even live in the same suburb." Now she understood how the system worked and she fastidiously laid the groundwork for each new project, addressing possible objections before they were raised. But that first failure still hurt.

All because of a lie.

With Travis's betrayal coming so soon after— their home deposit and some of the shelter's operating capital gone on his gambling addiction—it had almost broken her determination.

Jack covered her hand with his and gently squeezed. "Sometimes connections are a good thing."

His touch stole her breath and her train of thought. Easing her hand out of his, she raised her glass and drank, buying herself time.

"Winning because of who you know rather than through merit is wrong."

"So, would you prefer I didn't try to expedite the application? It would probably make a difference of only a couple of weeks. When did you say the bitsa is due to have her litter?"

Blast it, she'd forgotten about Lolly. Could the centre afford to keep her puppies if the litter was large? Julie considered the slender surplus that had to stretch to the end of the month. Without the extra income Jack had predicted from the doggie treat venture, Lolly and her pups were at risk. She couldn't allow the dogs to lose in the tug of war between principle and her conscience.

"Okay, Jack, I get your point. And . . . thanks for helping us."

Chapter Four

"Six weeks from idea to implementation must be some kind of record." Julie seemed pleased as she sorted notes and coins into her cashbox and looked at him. "Thanks for helping out at our grand opening today." Shade from the camphor laurel tree shifted with the breeze through the leaves, highlighting reddish-gold strands in her hair.

Jack closed the lid of the biscuit container and grinned at Julie. "That's the last box of oaties. We've got two tubs of love bones before we're sold out."

"Are you sure? Have we really sold everything else?" She lifted the lid of the nearest storage container, peered inside and dropped the lid. Shadows underlined her eyes and Jack guessed she'd been running on adrenaline as she had moved mountains setting up the project in such a short time.

They'd dined together almost every night since that first lunch meeting. What started as an excuse to get to know her better had thrown up several unexpected positives. Nora was expanding the vegetarian options on the pub menu and Julie had happily agreed to be the guinea pig.

'Why do we need a planning meeting *every* night, Jack?'

'Because we're setting this project up so quickly, we have to keep an eye on every detail. Two pairs of eyes are better than one, don't you agree?'

Manipulation wasn't his usual modus operandi and he half suspected she'd seen through his ruse, but heck, if it ensured she ate at least one decent meal a day, it was worth the minor deception. And he got to see her every day as she organised 'phase one' for the centre.

Just a week ago when he'd suggested doubling the number of boxes for their first takeaway treats stall, Julie had told him he was optimistic. At least that was his word for it. Julie's phrase had been more colourful. He persevered and she finally agreed.

'Bet we don't sell out or even come close.'

'What do you bet?' The words popped out of his mouth and his mind raced to catch up. Last night, he'd wanted to tease her out of her worries and being silly had won him two smiles and a mock punch.

She pinned him beneath her luminous blue gaze and stabbed her finger on the table. 'You seriously think we're going to sell everything? I'll eat my hat if we come close.' Despite her denial her blue eyes widened and hope flared in them. And right then the opportunity to lighten her worry morphed into desire to prove himself to her.

He leaned forward, captured her hand and linked their fingers. 'How about you agree to a mystery date with me? If we sell out, you're mine for the afternoon.'

Her fingers wiggled beneath his, and a spark of mischief glinted in her eyes. She lowered her voice to a sultry siren tone and leaned close as though they were conspirators plotting a coup. 'And if I win?'

'I'm yours to do with as you will.'

'Sounds like a win-win situation.' Her lips parted in that slow, secretive smile that had fuelled his sleep with X-rated dreams.

Julie handed over the last two boxes of love bones to a young mother who tucked them into a backpack squeezed into the low under-tray of the pram. A leash tied to the handle kept an elderly Labrador tucked in close and quiet beside her.

"We'll be here every Sunday from now on. Let

us know what you think of the treats." Julie smiled as she closed the cash box.

The woman rocked the pram and turned to the dog, "We'll be back. Goldie, come." The dog pushed to its feet and padded slowly beside her.

Jack unhooked their stall sign while Julie folded the cloth from the sales table. They reached for the lid of the plastic storage container at the same time. Her fingers brushed his and tingles of awareness ran up his arm.

"You first." Jack stood back and watched Julie pack the cash box and cloth.

"Your turn. I can't believe how successful we've been." She stretched her arms high and did a little jig.

Jack dropped the sign on top of the other gear and clipped the lid shut. He stood and caught hold of her hand and pulled her close. Eau de jasmine wafted around him, a scent he would always associate with Julie. In spite of the shadows beneath, her eyes were bright. "And that success now means—"

"Hmm, we get to celebrate with a drink at the pub?" She tilted her head and gave him a cheeky wink.

"Remember what I said last night? You're not planning to welsh on our bet, are you?" Maybe he should have considered how tired she'd be before he suggested Sunday afternoon and lined up Mick to cover his shift in the pub.

Because he had been confident of winning.

"If you're too tired, we can put it off until next weekend."

Please don't be tired.

She grinned. "I'm too intrigued to find out what you have planned. And you know what?"

"What?" On a high now she had agreed, his grin grew broader.

"Secretly, I hoped you'd win."

***

Julie opened the boot of Jack's black 4WD and lifted the first storage container.

"Let me do that." Jack reached for the container.

"It's empty, Jack. Like you said it would be." Like he'd promised. Jack had really helped her and the future looked brighter for the shelter.

"So?"

"I'm not a fragile hothouse flower. I lift weights at the gym and haul sacks of pet food around the shelter. And—it's empty." She balanced the handle on the tip of one finger and let the container swing. "See?"

"Just being a gentleman, but feel free." He stood aside and allowed her to grab two more empty storage containers and stow them before he lifted the heavy wooden slab that had served as their counter and slid it in to stand vertically beside the other gear.

Julie folded her arms and tipped her head to the side, following his movements.

"See something you like?" He turned and lifted both supports and stowed them. Hands on hips, he leaned against his car.

Her gaze flicked up to meet his. "Just admiring the view."

"Remind me, who won our bet?"

Julie sashayed over and spread her arms wide. "You won fair and square and here I am. So . . . what are you going to do about it?"

***

Cornflower-blue eyes regarded him and the moment stretched on as crowds of people strolled past, oblivious to the byplay between them. Oblivious to the fact all he wanted was to wrap her in his arms and kiss her. And not stop kissing her. In his mind, he could see his hands around her waist and he was lowering his head for a taste of her soft, pink mouth.

"Jack?"

He blinked as he realised he was holding her—close. When had he moved? Had she?

"Hey, if she's selling kisses, count me in."

Jack wrenched his attention back, drew a steadying breath and grinned at three young guys standing on the other side of the bright orange paint line marking the limits of their stall space. "Sorry, guys, sold out."

"Too bad." The tallest of the three punched the speaker's arm as they moved away.

Jack took Julie's arm and opened the passenger door. "Let's get out of here."

***

Julie stepped down onto the flat rock at the base of the waterfall and slipped off her shoes. "Of all the places you could have chosen, I didn't expect this. I haven't been in the National Park since I was a teenager."

Birds called from the tall trees along the ridge while below, water cut between rocks and flowed steadily out of a shallow pool. She sat on the edge of a naturally formed seat, enjoying the baking heat beneath her bottom. Summer heat, cool water, and a free afternoon in Jack's company—she couldn't ask for a better celebration. After rolling up each leg of her cargo pants she slid her feet into the clear water. Sucking in a breath, she wriggled her toes as the cold seeped into her feet. "It makes me feel alive."

It was the perfect place, her favourite type of relaxation. How had Jack known? She closed her eyes against the bright light and breathed in the scents of eucalyptus and summer-warmed flowers.

"Water not too cold?" Jack set his backpack down and toed off his joggers and joined her. "Hmm, deliciously cool." Citrus cologne mingled with the scent of eucalyptus and earth. Jack fit into this landscape so easily, as though he belonged here in the country.

Like he fits into my life. If she'd been able to make a 3-D print of her ideal man, Jack was the closest she'd come to achieving her wish list. Heck, she was certain he embodied the entire list and then some.

She shuffled sideways to make more room but when he sat, his thigh pressed along the length of hers. Delicious warmth contrasted with her cool toes, and his touch sent shivers of a different kind coursing through her. Her stomach tumbled and went into free fall and the rush of blood left her giddy. She peeked up at him.

Cinnamon-brown eyes glinted, and his arm enfolded her. "Come here. I'll keep you warm."

She turned into the furnace of Jack's chest and brushed her nose across his skin, seeking to imprint his scent in her memory. "I thought I'd lost our bet but this feels more like I've won."

His finger beneath her chin was callus-rough but his thumb was soft as he stroked her lower lip and tipped her head up. "Reckon we both have. Thanks for trusting me."

Trust? She did trust him, and she felt good about it. The knowledge that Travis hadn't killed her ability to believe in a good, decent man added a beautiful layer to an already red-letter day.

"About what?"

Soft as a butterfly wing, he brushed her mouth with his. She tasted warm mint on his breath before he drew back a little and met her gaze. "Everything, Julie. Running with my ideas, trusting me with your special project—and being a good sport."

"I never thought you had wicked intentions when you proposed that bet." But she hoped he wasn't planning to be entirely well behaved.

"Your trust means more than you know.

Although I won't say I haven't had an occasional wicked thought."

Tall, tanned, and totally trustworthy, Jack's words fired her imagination. Currents of heat raced through her, stealing her breath.

Wicked thoughts indeed.

"Can I *trust* you to act on at least some of them?"

***

Jack tucked a strand of hair behind Julie's ear and grinned at the sight of her kiss-swollen lips and half-closed eyes. What he wouldn't give to be able to take things to their natural conclusion. But this was neither the time nor the place. He eased the pressure of his arousal against his zipper and stood. Jeans were fine for working in the pub but not when he was kissing Julie.

He offered her a hand up. "Let's eat over in that patch of shade."

Hand-in-hand, they climbed the creek bank and strolled to a flattish area of pale grass. Jack spread a small, bright-red picnic blanket and unpacked the wicker hamper. He opened a bottle of sparkling wine and handed two glasses to Julie. At her raised eyebrow, he shrugged. "To celebrate. Would you like to do the honours?"

"Jack, you're so good at everything you do—"

"I aim to please." His gaze dropped to her lips. Soon he would do more than please her. Pleasure came to mind, and slow, soft seduction. Because with Julie, he was ten feet tall and he couldn't imagine leaving her. The speed with which he'd fallen for her should have alarmed his careful, guarded side—the numbers man who calculated everything to the nth degree. But working beside her today had confirmed his heart had joined the party. It felt wonderful.

"*That* was good too."

"Just good? I must be slipping for lack of practice."

She took the bottle and poured two glasses of wine before handing one to him. "We can work on that later . . . if you like."

Could he tell her about his father? Invested as he was in growing his relationship with Julie, would she change her mind when she knew his father's grand plan for his future in the capital? The plan he was more inclined than ever to dump.

Julie seemed to want stability and security here in her own town. All the things he'd been prepared to throw away when he struck out on his own now seemed—different when she was part of the equation. As their gazes connected, the heaviness in his chest lifted.

"Today should be fun. Let's leave the heavy stuff for later. Here's to a successful project—and the start of something wonderful."

Chapter Five

"Ms Aster?" A male voice called aloud, the pitch high as though he'd called several times, unsuccessfully.

Lost in memories that sent delicious tingles up her spine almost as good as Jack's kisses by the waterfall, Julie looked up from the bin of cat food. A man dressed in a dark brown business suit and peach tie stood on the other side of the glass that separated reception from the business side of the shelter. Wrenching her attention back to the fact she was at work, Julie replaced the lid and squirted anti-bacterial sanitiser on her hands, rubbing it in before hurrying through the door.

"Hello. I hope I didn't keep you waiting. How can I help you?"

He cleared his throat and peered nervously past her shoulder. Julie flicked a glance behind her.

Hunter, a large, grey and white cat with a tattered left ear, prowled along a high ledge running around the inside perimeter of the cattery. The cat sat and peered through the glass, green eyes wide and watchful, and slowly swished its tail. Intimidating and combative, Hunter was unlikely to make a match at the next showing but, thanks to the shelter's flourishing doggie treats business, they could afford to keep him for a while longer.

Julie turned her attention back to her visitor. "Hunter may not be handsome but he has a lot of character. Are you looking for a cat, Mr . . . "

He adjusted his tie and his Adam's apple bobbed up and down several times. "Clive Cavallier. Er, no, not a cat. Never a cat, Ms Aster. I was hoping to find a small dog."

"That's wonderful. And please call me Julie. I'll take you to the kennels. We have several smaller dogs available. You do know there is an adoption fee and—"

"Yes, yes. I know. Jack yammered in my ear for an hour or more when he brought in your application." Clive Cavallier's manner became more assured as she pulled the door to the cattery closed.

"Do you work at the local council office?"

"Yes, although I knew Jack previously. He was adamant I should come in and adopt an animal. Said I needed company now my wife has—" His nostrils flared and he marched ahead of her to the adjacent building.

Julie bit back the question she'd been about to ask and uttered a suitably general response. Pausing at the kennel door, she watched the man closely. "How much time can you give to an animal if you adopt one?"

"You should be glad someone wants to adopt one of your strays. I don't think—"

Tamping down a rush of anger at his use of 'strays', Julie reached for calm. Vetting prospective owners was sometimes tricky when all they wanted was to point to 'the one' and take it home immediately. "Mr Cavallier . . . Clive . . . I ask because the amount of time you have available will give me some idea of which animal might best suit your lifestyle. I have no wish to pry."

He blinked and looked down at the ground. "I'm sorry. I have too much free time since my wife walked out. Plenty of time to play and walk a dog. Jack told me to move on and get another dog. My ex-wife took Tiddles and . . . well, it's a bit lonely. Jack is right but he can be quite—*compelling* when he decides he knows what's best. But look who I'm talking to."

"What do you mean?" Compelling was a good

word to describe Jack's manner. A great word for him. Few people could have got her to move from caution to action as quickly as Jack when it came to the new venture. Elemental energy zapped through him and swept everyone along for the ride.

She held the door open and followed Clive inside. Excited barking rose several decibels as they entered the hub.

"Well, he knows how these things work. The payment he made to have your application fast-tracked saw it jump to the head of the queue."

"Payment?" Her hand clung to the metal latch of the inner door. Of course she remembered Jack raising the possibility of using his connections at council to speed up the processing of the shelter's application but there'd been no further mention of money. Nor had there been any such item listed on the financial statement he'd drawn up for her. Flutters of unease battered the walls of her stomach.

"Jack's accountancy firm backed the shelter's application. You're lucky to have him underwriting your venture. That sort of cachet opens most doors."

Unease turned to lead pellets.

Jack lied.

About who he was and about what she could achieve on her own. He'd let her think her application had been accepted on its own merits but he'd greased its path. He didn't really believe in her.

Not only that, but his friend said Jack was an accountant. Not a receiver. It didn't make sense. Why would an accountant be working in a pub?

Who is Jack?

The kennel's warmth failed to keep the chill of disappointment and disillusion at bay.

Jack *lied.*

Beside Clive Cavallier, a small white ball of fluff yapped and thrust her nose through the bars. He pointed at Bonnie, the smallest of their rescue pets. "What about that one?"

***

Jack knocked a second time on Julie's front door, rocked back on his heels and shoved his hands deep into his pockets. After a cloudless day, the thermometer had risen and leaves hung limp on camphor laurels lining the street. The air was still and heavy, with a sense of waiting. For what, Jack had no idea.

Inside Julie's house, lights burned. On the other side of the door, Anna whined and scratched at the panel but still Julie didn't appear. Thirteen voice mail messages over three days without a reply from her was more than enough reason for this late night visit. He wasn't leaving without checking she was safe and well.

Jack didn't think he was being bigheaded, but what Julie and he had shared by the waterfall hadn't been casual. Dammit, it had meant something special. They had a connection he was certain wasn't one-sided.

So he knocked a third time, called, and then headed down the side of the old Queensland style house. His foot hit the bottom tread at the same time as Anna burst through the dog flap and padded down the wooden stairs. She shoved her nose into his hand and whined.

He stroked her head and looked into her gentle, brown eyes. "Hi, girl. Where's your mistress? Where's Julie?"

Anna barked before trotting towards the front yard. She stopped and looked back at Jack.

"You want me to follow you? Okay, let's go find Julie." Maybe he should be heading off to the shelter rather than following Anna. He wanted answers, preferably face-to-face so he could read her expression. His hand reached for his phone and he hit the speed dial button then as quickly thumbed the end call. Why would she answer a phone call when she'd ignored thirteen texts?

As Anna led Jack around the corner, a strong easterly wind arrived, picking up dust and stinging his cheeks. When the dog crossed the road and padded along an unfamiliar track that cut through bushland, a sinking feeling hit his stomach. But when they emerged at the rear of the animal shelter, lights shone from inside the kennel. Inside, a dog howled, the sound filled with pain.

He stopped beside the rear door and peered through the safety glass panel. Julie's gentle, encouraging voice rose and fell beyond the inner wall of the central hub. Without thinking, he pressed down on the handle. The door was locked. He rapped sharply on the glass. "Julie, it's me, Jack."

"I'm busy. Go away." Her voice sounded raspy and annoyed, but at least she was there. It was a start after three days of silence.

He rapped again. "We need to talk. Open up."

She stood and pushed the hub door open with her bottom and walked towards him, hands raised and bloody. With her elbow, she pushed the lever handle down and the door swung open outwards. "Shut the door. You're letting in the dust." Ignoring him, she returned to the animal in distress behind the hub wall.

Jack followed, shutting the inner door softly behind him. Lying on blood-soaked bedding lay the bitsa Julie had worried about. Three newborn puppies blindly nuzzled their mother's belly while Julie focused on a fourth being born. Julie crooned to the mother. "You're doing very well, Lolly. Good girl, good girl."

Jack stood watching her expertly deliver the pup. "Can I do anything?"

"Grab that towel and wrap this little guy." Red-eyed, she threw him a look of grudging thanks. Whatever lay beneath her reluctance he planned to uncover as soon as her hands weren't preoccupied with the puppies.

"Can you tell how many pups she has?" Fascinated in spite of the late hour and the driving need to reconnect with Julie, Jack watched as she gently felt Lolly's belly and spoke in soothing tones. Her concern for the dog's pain touched him.

She cared so much about the animals under her care and tried so hard to find them good homes. Even Clive had commented in a way that sent a surge of jealousy through Jack. The feeling surprised him, not because he was jealous but because the emotion was so strong.

Yes, Clive was a free agent since Marla had walked out on him. So was Julie. And she was pissed off with Jack for a reason he couldn't fathom.

They worked steadily together until six puppies lay beside their mother. Julie cleaned her hands on a towel and wiped her forearm over her sweaty brow. She pushed slowly to her feet. "That's it. They'll need checking on every—"

If he hadn't been watching her closely, he would have missed the sudden draining of colour from her face. He caught her as she crumpled in his arms. "Julie?" He carried her out of the hub and lowered her gently onto a chair beside the reception counter.

As he brushed hair off her forehead he swore beneath his breath. Cold and clammy beneath his hand, she moaned.

"You're sick. Why didn't you get the vet in, or one of the other staff? Why didn't you tell me?" More angry with himself that he hadn't made the effort to check on her sooner, he filled a paper cup at the water cooler and carried it back to her. "Here, sip this."

"Everyone was otherwise occupied. No one else could come when Lolly went into labour." Julie struggled to sit up. Her hand shook as she raised the cup to her mouth and Jack steadied her hold. She sipped and then slumped back in the seat. "Have to see to the puppies. Have to—"

"You have to go to bed. I'll phone the doctor."

"But the puppies—"

"No buts. I'll look after them. In fact, I have a great idea."

***

Dr Jensen closed his medical bag with two sharp clicks. "Normally I'd put a patient suffering like this into hospital, but if you're sure you can stay? Don't you have a pub to run?"

Jack leaned against the doorjamb. "I'll call Mick in to take over my shifts. Between him and Nora and the new barman, it will be fine." Aside from which Julie was his number one priority. Number two barked from her bed in the laundry.

"Sounds like you'll have your hands full. I'll see myself out."

Jack heard the front door shut as he stood beside Julie's bed. She was pale, with shadows like bruises beneath her closed eyes, but her breathing had settled into a regular pattern after the doctor had given her an injection. But while she was ill, he had every intention of staying by her side.

At least, until she was strong enough to tell him just what the hell had happened between those kisses by the waterfall and now.

Pre-dawn lightened the sky. Hating to see her vibrant nature dimmed by illness, Jack sat on the edge of the bed and held her hand. It was cool, but her skin had lost the clamminess of last night. She mumbled something and he leaned closer, trying to make out her words.

"Lolly."

"She's fine and so are her pups. They're in good hands." Typical. As sick as she was, Julie's first thought was of the dog she'd been caring for. Jack stroked her cheek and her eyelids fluttered open. She turned her head towards his hand, and sighed before closing her eyes.

His heart thumped with joy. It didn't matter they'd met only weeks ago. It didn't matter that she hadn't returned his messages. In illness, Julie had turned to him. She'd seemed comforted by his presence. Whatever was wrong, he would fix it and move forward.

With her.

Several short barks brought his attention back to his second patient. He dropped a soft kiss on Julie's forehead and tucked her hand beneath the sheet. Then he padded softly down the hall to the laundry.

Opening the door a crack, he peered into the small room. Lolly lay on her side with five pups suckling from her teats. The sixth, the runt of her litter, was out in the cold. Jack scooped up the tiny ball of hair and gently eased him into position so he, too, could feed. "There you go, champ. Nothing wrong with you that a good feed won't fix."

He refilled the water bowl, and set out biscuits for Lolly before carrying a second bowl out to where Anna slept in the enclosed back veranda. She raised her head and whined what sounded like a question.

He hunkered down and stroked her soft ears and head. "You really do talk, don't you, girl? Your mistress will be fine. And when she's better, we're going to make some ground rules. Guess what number one will be?"

Anna yipped and Jack grinned. "Got it in one. We share everything, the good, the bad, and the ugly. Communication, that's the key."

Chapter Six

"No, I don't want to talk about it." Julie tugged the sheet higher, crossed her arms over her chest and stared through her bedroom window. Perhaps she was being childish—okay, she knew she was—and she knew for certain that her manner was ungracious. But Jack had lied. Nothing excused that.

Jack placed a chair beside her bed, and sat with Lolly's smallest pup cradled in his lap. He stroked its soft fur while watching Julie closely. "I'm not going anywhere until you tell me why you didn't answer my texts. Correct me if I'm wrong but I thought we had achieved a level of trust. I shared things I'm not in the habit of telling casual acquaintances. And I thought you'd done the same."

There was no getting around the fact he had left his work at the pub to care for her and the new puppies. She owed him an explanation, no matter how reluctant she was to have this conversation. And it was clear he wasn't going to leave without her spelling it out for him. She clenched her hands in her lap and met his gaze. "You crossed a line when you lied to me."

Jack stiffened and his gaze lost focus, as though replaying a conversation sentence by sentence, word by word. Finally, he shook his head. "What lie do you think I told?"

"You lied by omission. It's as bad as if you spoke it."

Jack frowned. "I have no idea what you're talking about."

A needle of doubt pricked her certainty. From their first meeting, she had sensed Jack was honourable. Sincere, dependable—all of which had made his betrayal so bad.

Had she misunderstood? Had she somehow got things wrong?

She swallowed against the sore throat that swelled uncomfortably as her emotions threatened to overwhelm her. Ticking almost every box on her wish list, Jack had seemed like the real deal, her ideal man. Discovering he had feet of clay and could lie to her had seemed so much worse after the high of their successful project.

So much worse after the afternoon they'd spent celebrating. Getting to know one another on a whole new level.

Opening up to him had felt right at the time, but allowing herself to daydream about a future with Jack had been stupid. She pressed her teeth into her lower lip, and sniffed back equally stupid tears that threatened to fall.

"Clive Cavallier told me. Were you ever going to tell me you're an accountant? Or that your company paid a bribe to facilitate the shelter's application through council?"

Jack's knuckles turned white and his fingers dug into the arm of the chair. When his shoulders slumped, Julie's doubts grew. He didn't look guilty. He didn't look embarrassed or even angry. One emotion radiated from him and it wasn't the one she had expected. Jack was—hurt.

"I have never lied to you. I am an accountant."

"You said you were a receiver working at the pub."

"That's one of the jobs accountants do. It's a relief to get out of the office occasionally." Softly, he stroked the puppy's head.

"Oh." Had she jumped to a conclusion—the *wrong* conclusion—about the money he'd paid to the council as well? The possibility horrified her but she had to know.

"The payment you made to council? Was that a—?"

"Bribe? No, Julie. I thought you knew me better than that." He rose from his chair and carried the puppy back to its mother. When he returned, his gaze was sad.

"Most applicants pay a standard fee and are prepared to wait the prescribed period. If an application is urgent, and you can find the money, you pay a fee on top of the regular one to have your paperwork expedited. A *fee*, not a bribe. It's simple really.

"Each year, my firm chooses a local community group to support. I chose yours. Paying the fee was part of our commitment to supporting the work you do. Which we will continue to support, regardless of—"

He shrugged and stepped through the doorway.

He was going. He would walk down her hallway and out of her life. She was sure she would never see him again. Words lodged in her throat and her voice cracked. "Jack, I'm sorry."

He half looked over his shoulder. "So am I."

There wasn't enough air. She rubbed a hand over her aching chest. How could she have made those accusations? Didn't she know him better than to jump to a stupid conclusion? He had shown her in every possible way that she could depend on him and trust him, and she knew he cared about her.

As much as I care about him?

The sound of his footsteps receded towards the back of the house before a door closed softly.

***

Jack raised the axe and brought it down with a thud that echoed off Julie's shed wall. Physical exercise hadn't helped him sleep and a twinge in his calf muscles was all he had to show for the fifteen-kilometre run he'd taken after leaving her house.

Bear padded up, nudged him and gently tugged on the leg of his jeans.

"What is it, old fella? Time to check on Lolly again?"

Bear licked his hand, but even the touch of his canine best friend's wet nose and raspy tongue failed to ease the dull ache in his chest. But he couldn't leave the puppies, or Julie until she had recovered enough to care for the pups.

He knew he shouldn't feel this unhappy. But after their picnic by the falls, he'd been sure Julie was *the one*. Deciding to stay in town and make a new life had been a no-brainer. Fool that he was, he'd even found himself studying house and land packages in the real estate agent's window. A future here with Julie had seemed more than likely. More of a certainty.

Until last night.

At the first suggestion of doubt, she'd believed a stranger rather than him. The evidence of his success hadn't been enough. He put the axe away and stacked a pile of firewood for Julie's pot-belly stove in the garden shed. He'd imagined sitting beside her in front of the fire when winter came. Now . . .

"Come on, Bear. Let's see to those pups." Heavy-footed, he trudged to the house.

"Jack?" Julie stood at the top of the back stairs, white knuckles gripping the railing. Flushed cheeks and bright eyes were still the only spots of colour.

"What's wrong? You shouldn't be out of bed." He took the stairs two at a time.

She reached for him, and an unspoken question hovered between them.

He took her hand and slipped an arm around her

waist. She pressed closer and looked up at him. Her lips parted and a need to press his mouth to hers rose strong within him. In spite of her lack of trust, he wanted to mend fences. Somehow they would find a way around the rift that lay between them.

A shiver passed through her and she leaned against him, her head resting on his shoulder.

Hair tickled his cheek and he closed his eyes, breathing in her floral shampoo. It was hard to recapture his annoyance and indignation when she was in his arms. Hard to remember why his life plans had come apart at the seams when she stood by him. And yet . . .

He poked a mental finger in his chest. She hadn't trusted him.

She tipped her head and met his gaze. "I got it so wrong and I'm sorry. For doubting you, and for believing, even for a single second, that you'd lie. It's probably too late but I want you to know how much your help meant to me."

Too late? To apologise, or did she mean for them?

She cupped his cheek with warm fingers. "You're the best man I've ever met. Just remember that." Julie shivered again.

"Come inside. You should be in bed." He led her inside and shut the back door.

"I wanted to explain before—" She ran her tongue across cracked lips. "I was naïve when I started at the shelter. I trusted my ex and I lost animals because I was too trusting. He gambled away our money and then took some from the shelter account. We were on the verge of closing down.

"Then you showed up with a dozen ideas and asked me to trust you. Having you on our side, all the things you did for me—us—well, it felt unreal, like a beautiful bubble. When Clive said those things, I thought the bubble had burst. I let the past overshadow what I knew to be true about you . . ."

He knew she'd been in a relationship with someone called Travis, but not that the man had done the dirty on her. No wonder she'd been leery when she'd thought another man had abused her trust.

Wishing he'd known all the details of Julie's breakup with her ex earlier, he touched his forehead to hers. Knowing only half the story, he hadn't realised the effect that betrayal had had on her. "I get it. Trust is a two-way street. I burred up and didn't think about what you'd been through. Losing animals like that must have been hard."

"Yet despite how I treated you, you stayed and took care of me." Her lashes fluttered down and she lowered her head against his chest.

"Of course. Look, we need to have a full and open conversation, but you won't get better if you don't go back to bed and rest." He slipped an arm around her shoulders and gently drew her towards the hallway.

If their next conversation led where he hoped it would, he knew exactly which block of land he wanted to show her first. He kissed her forehead.

She uttered a soft sigh and melted against him, forcing him to stop.

"But you need to go back to bed. I'll make a cuppa and—"

She pulled away, an extra layer of pink colouring her cheeks. "Oh dear. I almost forgot. You have visitors. Nora sent them over from the pub."

Voices rose from the direction of the lounge room, not the radio as he'd first thought. "Who is it?"

Softly, she squeezed his hand and drew him forward. "Just come and see."

Jack dropped his arm around her waist as they walked slowly down the hall. They entered the living room and the last two people he expected to see in Julie's home looked up. "Dad, Mum, what are you doing here?"

The deep crease above his father's hawk-like nose sent waves of disquiet rushing through Jack's gut. 'You're a disappointment to me', it proclaimed like an exclamation mark.

"Really, Jack, I'd expect you to be happy to see your mother and me after we've driven all this way just to see you." There it was, the 'you've let us down again' tone his father had perfected during Jack's childhood. The accusation of ingratitude was still able to draw figurative blood.

Beside him, Julie drew a soft breath and took a step away. "I'll put the kettle on."

His arm tightened on her hip. "There's no need to go. Nothing my parents have to say to me needs privacy." He drew her to sit down beside him on the two-seater sofa.

His mother pinned her 'reasonable' smile in place and rested her hands in her lap. "We want you back home, dear. I miss you so much."

His father's dark grey suit jacket swung open as he thrust his head forward and pinned Jack with a glacial glare. "When are you going to give up this nonsense and do your duty by your family? We've been very accommodating in giving you time out of the office, but playing at being a receiver is beneath you. A Schultz doesn't get his hands dirty."

A pulse throbbed in Jack's temple as familiar anger roiled in his gut. "Do you think I've failed? The pub is ready for resale and the figures are looking very good."

"Of course you haven't failed, dear. But your father could use your help in the business and—"

His father sat back and slapped his hands on the arms of the chair. "Then your *work* here is done and it's time to knuckle down."

"To a real job, you mean? Dad, this is just more of the same argument. I told you before I left Brisbane, I don't want to be stuck in an office all the time."

"But, dear, you're so good at what you do." His mother's eyes gleamed with unshed tears as she cast a furtive glance at Julie. And at Jack's hand curled around Julie's waist.

He'd bet his eye teeth she was already counting grandchildren and planning future visits up the Range.

"Thanks, Mum. And I promise to visit often.

With Julie." Unsure if he imagined her soft gasp, he took her left hand in his and squeezed gently.

"I'm sure Ms Aster recognises duty is more important than personal wishes." His father's philosophy had guided Jack's choice of profession but he'd be damned if it ruled his life.

Before he could open his mouth, Julie faced his father. "Actually, Mr Schultz, being happy at work makes for better workers, and lowers stress levels. Perhaps you don't know all the good Jack has done for our community and for our animal rescue centre in the short time he's been here?"

"He's got the tavern up and running. Isn't that enough playing?" His father thrust a belligerent jaw forwards.

"Hardly playing, Dad. But maybe there's a solution to make us both happy. We could open an office here. There's plenty of work and I could do an occasional stint as a receiver. What do you think?" He had no idea where the loosely formed suggestion came from but it took root and grew as he waited for his father's reaction. A base in town, easy access to Western and Central Queensland when a business required his special skills—

Julie shifted on the seat beside him, her leg brushing his.

Not too often or too long away from home. Not if Julie's waiting for me

Chapter Seven

The following summer - one year on

"Ready on the mike, Jack?" Julie looked up at her fiancé standing on the dais they had constructed as part of the renovations of the café in the park. Jack's ideas and energy had taken the shelter well into the black and the past six months had seen numerous improvements. But this was her favourite.

He grinned and leaned down for a quick kiss. "Ready. I'll give you ten seconds then I'll begin."

Giggling more than Marsha at her teenage worst, Julie raced around the side of the building and gave a signal to her staff. ". . . three, two, one."

From the dais, Jack's whisky-smooth voice launched into the introduction. "Ladies and gentlemen, boys and girls, welcome to the Second Chance Café . . . "

Clapping and children's excited squeals greeted Marsha as she paraded the first two dogs along the 'red carpet', the teenager's own idea for the café's opening. Julie breathed a sigh of relief. Over-the-top ideas weren't her thing but the celebrity approach seemed to be a hit.

Doug shuffled his feet, ready to follow Marsha. Four exuberant puppies strained on their leads but Doug held them with a calm Julie applauded. Having Doug as her new second-in-charge had lightened her workload considerably. When she and Jack left on their honeymoon in a few weeks, she knew he'd handle management tasks well. Handling Marsha might be more of a challenge.

The teen sashayed off the red carpet and winked at Doug as she passed. "Your turn, Doug. Go wow the ladies with Delia's litter of babies 'cos they sure won't be wowed by you."

Smothering a chuckle, Julie opened the gate. "They're looking good, Doug. Okay, Delia's puppies next." Doug threw Marsha a look that promised words would be exchanged as soon as he returned and then strolled onto the carpet.

A dark-haired woman approached the enclosure, leading a boisterous young dog and pushing a pram with a toddler chattering excitedly.

"Hi, Lisa. How's Ally doing?" Julie squatted and patted the sole female of Lolly's litter last year. Budman, the runt of the litter and Jack's little buddy, now resided with her and Jack, Anna and Bear on their new farm a few kilometres to the north of the city.

"She's wonderful. After Goldie passed away, I didn't think I could face having another dog but Ally stole my heart. And my slippers, the TV remote, a library book, and ran away with my brand-new, knit top and tried to bury it. But I wouldn't be without her." Lisa rocked the pram while her toddler made a grab at Ally's ear.

"Good to see you're all settled."

"Thanks, Julie. I hope those puppies out there find homes today too." Lisa headed off down the path. With luck, most of the rescued animals would make a match today.

The morning parade rolled on and Julie answered questions, filled in paperwork, and made arrangements for transfers of matched pets.

At last, Jack was delivering his closing thanks. "The next parade will be in three months, right here at the Second Chance Café. Tell your friends and see you then."

Julie handed a set of registration papers to Doug and he led the last adopting family away to collect their new pet. Stretching her arms above her head, she squealed when Jack's hands slid around her waist and lifted her from her seat.

"What about you? Let's see—glorious hair, healthy skin, good teeth, adorable eyes . . . You suit my wish list perfectly. Can I take you home with me?"

"What wish list? You work everything out by the numbers." Sliding her arms around Jack's neck, she kissed his chin. "You're my maestro of math. None of this would have happened without your mad skills, Jack Schultz. You don't make wishes; you fulfil them."

Brushing his nose against hers, Jack kissed the tip and then laid a path of soft kisses all the way to her ear. "I have a wish list. It started the day I met you."

Her pulse kicked up a notch as it did every time he touched her. Thinking of her own wish list for the first time in months, she knew Jack had blown it out of the water. What more could she want than the rest of her life with this gorgeous man? "So, have you ticked off every item or is the last one our wedding?"

"I'm nowhere near ticking off everything."

Surprised and a little disappointed, Julie leaned back in his arms. "But the idea of a wish list is to tick off each item as you achieve it."

"Ah, well, there's the problem. You see, each day I spend with you, I wish for another like it. My wish list will never end because I'll always want more time with you. Every day, a new wish—to spend another day, and all our lives together."

"Oh, Jack."

He lifted her off her feet and swung her round. As her feet touched the ground, he gave her a heart-melting, breath-stealing, pulse-spiking look. "But we could sneak off home now and cross off one of today's wishes. Coming?"

The End

Short and Sweet: 3

When You Wish

Susanne Bellamy

Chapter 1

Peering through rising mist, Nate Greenwood took the bend in the road more slowly than usual. He'd passed one car on this quiet stretch of back road and, of course, it had flicked up a chunk of stone that took out one headlight.

Good old Murphy's Law.

The lone headlight picked out grey-edged puddles and piles of slush along the muddy shoulder and the ragged line of bitumen glistened darkly with melted snow. Nate shivered and cranked up the heater another degree. Maybe he should have waited until morning to drive up to Snow King Lodge for his meeting, but beating the traffic and getting out of the city on a Thursday night had seemed like a good idea.

He glanced at the digital display on his dashboard: 7:45 p.m. The hotel had promised to hold his room, no matter how late he arrived. Driving to the conditions had made the trip slower than expected, but even at this speed, he'd still make it with time to grab a late meal—

A strange noise in the engine caught his attention. He turned off his *Queen* DVD to listen. Odd noises combined with the fact his one remaining headlight seemed to be growing dimmer spelled trouble.

No, no, no . . .

Certain it meant his alternator was failing, Nate groaned. Breaking down in the middle of nowhere wasn't part of his plan. He was good at making plans, following plans, sticking to his plans. Excellence in planning was his strength.

Even his decision to take this quiet back road had been carefully considered to avoid the rush of skiers keen to hit the snowfields and ski the first decent snowfall of winter. But it was *not* worth the risk of missing the meeting with J. Thomas Spencer.

Call it what it is: an interview.

Spencer's HR man had reached out to him after the awards ceremony, and when the top engineering design company reached out hot on the heels of his *Best Innovative Design* win . . . well, Nate knew headhunting when he saw it.

He checked the GPS display, and realised it had been static for the past few kilometres. Now he thought about it, it hadn't moved since he came through the narrow, winding pass. He glanced at his phone display on the dashboard—no reception. "Just great. In a dead spot with a dying alternator. Can anything else go wrong tonight?"

Venting his frustration focused him on his problem. "Every problem has a solution," he muttered as he drove along the single lane strip of bitumen, keeping an eye open for signs of a driveway. He'd passed through the small town of Denby Crossing several kilometres back, before the car climbed towards the pass. Getting back to the town would be impossible if the alternator failed. Steep mountain road, sharp bends, no headlights—recipe for disaster. No, the best he could hope for was a farmhouse with a landline.

Faint muddy tyre tracks appeared on the road, curving in his direction. Nate felt like fist pumping in relief but settled for turning onto the graded driveway. Swirling mist and lack of a driver's side headlight obscured the details of a sign behind the wire fence. Preferring not to stop and check in case the alternator finally died, he crossed his fingers that the driveway led to a farm and not something like an unmanned electricity substation.

Bumping down the road, night and mist pressed in all around. Through shifting clouds of grey on black, he glimpsed a light—there, and then gone so quickly he wasn't sure it was real. The dim headlight picked up what looked like a neatly tended hedge before fading to nothing.

Darkness descended. Nate braked gently, trying to recall if there were any obstacles like trees ahead as he rolled to a stop. Grateful his speed had been little more than running pace, he switched the ignition off and sat, dragging in a breath. The action of unclipping the phone from its holder lit up the screen. In the darkness all around him, it was blinding. He tipped the phone face down and unclipped his seat belt. Time to investigate if he'd seen the light of a farmhouse or if the headlight had simply reflected off something.

He turned on the torch app and explored along the hedge until he found an old-fashioned gate of chicken wire in a rusting metal frame. It opened onto a brick pathway that split around a circular garden, bare in the middle of winter, and ended at the foot of a shallow set of stairs. He peered into the darkness. The house appeared to be a low-set stone building with a shallow open veranda.

As he set a foot on the lowest stone tread, a dog's soft growl sounded from behind the closed door. He raised his phone and the torchlight reflected off a polished ship's bell. Tugging the cord produced a sharp ting, but, for good measure, he knocked on the door. From the other side the growling rumbled on and he imagined a working dog sitting there, staring at the door and picking up his scent.

A light came on inside, shining softly through a leadlight panel that filled the upper third of the door. Above his head a security light flickered on, bathing him in clear white light.

"Who's there?" The female voice was young, and a little high-pitched. "Good girl, sit."

Nate cleared his throat. "Hi, sorry to bother you but my car has broken down and I don't have any phone reception. Could I use your phone to call for roadside assistance please?"

Through the coloured pieces of glass he could just make out the shape of a head. A silver-rimmed circle below the leadlight panel cued him in. Mentally, he applauded the safety consciousness of the woman who was checking him out through a peephole.

"Are you alone?"

"Yes." He moved aside hoping she could see there was no one with him.

A lock clicked, the door opened the length of a safety chain and the snout of a handsome Border Collie poked through, quivering and sniffing him. One blue and one brown eye assessed him. Above the dog, a pair of wary blue eyes looked him over, looked past him and back to meet his gaze. The door closed, the chain rattled and then the woman opened the door wide.

"Come in." She stood back, but maintained a careful distance.

She was older than the impression her voice had first given him, maybe in her late twenties, with hair the colour of chestnuts. A smattering of freckles lay across her nose and cheeks, drawing attention to eyes that watched his every move as he wiped his shoes on a bristled doormat.

"No need to take your shoes off."

He stepped into a carpeted hallway. Although warmer than outside once the door closed behind him, it was still cool and he shivered, grateful for the reprieve from the icy air. He'd had the car heater cranked up high, but the temperature was plummeting and more snow was forecast. "I hope I didn't get you out of bed?"

She wore a purple dressing gown, but shook her head and led the way into a cosy room. A log fire—a real one, he noted with surprise and genuine pleasure—burned in the fireplace. The wood-panelled room was simply furnished but comfortable. Two old-fashioned leather armchairs were angled towards the fire, and heavy red curtains were drawn across two windows, although a narrow gap between one pair might have been responsible for the light he'd glimpsed.

"Have a seat by the fire. I'll pop the kettle on. Would you like a hot drink?"

"I don't want to be a nuisance."

"I was just about to make one anyway. Tea, coffee?"

"Coffee please, white, no sugar. Thanks. Do you mind if I call roadside assistance from your phone?"

She gestured to a small dark wooden desk in the corner behind the door. "Be my guest."

Turning to the young dog, she raised one hand. "Stay, Crackles."

Crackles sat across the doorway when she left the room, observing Nate as he warmed his hands at the fire and looked back at the dog watching him. When his hands were warm again, he rose from in front of the fire.

The dog gave a low rumbling growl.

"Okay, Crackles, I'm just going to use the phone." Slowly Nate walked towards the desk. The dog followed his every movement as he reached for the handset. It was outdated technology but clearly necessary. He'd forgotten there were so many places that still didn't have reliable mobile reception. In the city, he took such conveniences for granted.

Holding the phone to his ear, he glanced at a small pile of mail while he listened for a dial tone. A yellow envelope lay on top of the pile, its top edge slit and a letter opener lying nearby, but it was the address that caught his attention:

Santa Claus

North Pole

The Earth

It was so unexpected that he blinked and picked up the envelope, as though proximity would somehow change the childish handwriting to the name of this property—whatever it was called.

Nope—the addressee remained the same. He thought of his GPS position, or lack thereof, and chuckled softly. *I was driving off the map. Maybe I've landed at Santa's secret headquarters in the southern hemisphere?*

Realising that no sound was coming through the phone pressed to his ear and with his hopes sinking, he dropped the envelope and tapped the handset buttons several times. Still nothing. He tapped the phone against his free hand then jiggled the white plastic buttons again.

The woman returned carrying a tray with two steaming mugs and a plate of small cakes decorated with pink icing and sprinkles.

She set the tray on the desk and met his gaze. "Did you get through?"

He shook his head and returned the phone to the cradle. "Maybe the line's down."

"It happens from time to time up here apparently. Cake?" She offered the plate of cakes.

Without thinking, he took one and accepted the blue mug whose handle she turned towards him. "Does that *apparently* mean you haven't lived here for long?"

She gave him a sharp gaze. "This is my first winter up here. I'm Sophie Denby. Crackles, you've already met. I'll make up a bed for you. There's nothing we can do about your car tonight."

"My name's Nate Greenwood." He set the coffee mug down, held out a hand and shook hers. Her hand was small and warm and totally engulfed by his. "That's kind of you to offer, but are you okay with opening your house to a stranger?"

She tipped her head to one side and met his gaze. "Crackles will be sleeping outside your door. I think that should cover both of our concerns, don't you?"

Chapter 2

After settling her unexpected guest into the spare bedroom, Sophie Denby read the address on the yellow envelope and frowned.

Flipping the envelope over, she read the sender's name and address again: *Jackson Milton* from *Denby Crossing.* Her home and old stomping ground before she'd bought Wishfort Farm. Her misreading of the name in the realtor's window as 'Wish for it' had been the reason she'd noticed the ad in the first place. Possibilities conjured by the improbable name had led her here.

Nate's arrival had prevented her reading the newly opened letter. Wondering who Jackson Milton was, what he was wishing for and how his letter had landed in her letterbox, in her mind she heard Gran's voice: *Do you think you're telepathic or something? Get on and open it!*

Chuckling at the power Gran exerted even when she wasn't in the same house, let alone the same room,

Sophie extracted the letter, opened the folded page and read the carefully printed writing of a young boy.

Dear Santa

My name is Jackson Milton. I'm 8 and mum and dad sed Ricky (my little brother he's 5) won't get to see you again because he wont be here at Crismus but he rekons you will fly in to see him. He ~~beleiv belives~~ knows you can do anything even visit when it isnt Crismus. Please come. Thats all i want for Crismus.

I promise I wont ask for anything els if you just come now.

Signed Jackson Milton

ps can you bring Rudolf? Ricky loves his toy Rudolf

Sophie sank onto the edge of her armchair and stared into the fire without seeing its flickering flames. A lump of sadness for the unknown child filled her throat. Was he truly so ill that he wouldn't be alive come Christmas? She needed to talk to Dave at the Denby Post Office and find out more about the family. They must have arrived after she left town or she'd have known all about them. That was the thing about small towns; everyone knew everything about everybody.

Her cheeks heated at the reminder. Despite the

way she'd left Denby, one thing was clear in her mind: she was meant to make Jackson's wish for his brother happen.

The only problem was how?

Setting the letter back on her desk, she switched off the lights and headed to her bedroom, climbed into bed and set her feet on the hot water bottle. How on earth could she fly Santa in—*with Rudolph*—to fill Jackson's dream for his little brother? Confident that it was Dave who had slipped the letter to Santa into her post office box, she made a mental note to phone him and find out more about the Milton family as soon as the phone line was fixed.

But as she snuggled under the doona, her thoughts veered off towards her unexpected houseguest.

Nate Greenwood was good-looking, with impeccable manners that Gran would appreciate. Her gran maintained one never knew if first impressions were accurate, but there was something reassuring in the way Nate had questioned whether she was okay with him staying in her house.

She wasn't. Men in general were still on her don't-touch-with-a-bargepole list. Uncomfortable with inviting a stranger into her home, she'd seriously considered sending him with a pile of blankets to sleep in the barn. But the forecast was for more snow overnight, and the barn would be freezing. She wouldn't turn anyone away in this weather.

Or maybe one man would get shown the door.

Her ex could take a flying jump and— no, she'd let even him stay. But *he* could freeze his lying arse off . . . in the barn.

Maybe Nate was different, but it didn't matter. Once he was settled in, she'd left Crackles outside his door.

Meeting his gaze—grey-blue eyes the colour of stormy summer clouds—had decided her. Grannie Annie held the view that you could tell much about a person by the way they met your eyes. His gaze was open and steady, and the invitation had popped out of her mouth.

"I hope you're right about that, Gran," she whispered, turning to the window.

Snow began to fall, silent and barely visible in the faint light of a sickle moon, newly risen above the crest of the hills. If tonight's snowfall was heavy, how much longer would it take a repair crew to fix her phone line?

And how was she to get her unexpected guest

back to Denby when her car was in for repairs? She rolled onto her side and let the falling snow lull her to sleep. That piece of bad news she would share with Nate in the morning.

Chapter 3

As soon as Nate woke, he dressed warmly, opened the bedroom door and looked around for Crackles. The dog was out of sight, but the aroma of bacon sizzling led him to the kitchen. He stood in the doorway and took in the old-fashioned kitchen with its big cast-iron stove.

Sophie stood in front of the range wielding a pair of tongs over a pan.

Crackles yipped, and the sound of it seemed friendly enough that Nate stepped into the room.

Sophie turned and smiled, but it was reserved and a little self-conscious.

"Good morning. Breakfast is almost ready, coffee's on the bench by the window." She tucked a strand of hair behind her ear and turned back to the frying pan. She picked up a plate and began filling it with bacon and eggs then stopped and looked at him. "You aren't vegetarian, are you?"

"No and that's very kind, but you shouldn't have

put yourself out for me." Nate poured coffee into a mug and pondered how he could express his gratitude before he went on his way. His eye fell on an almost-empty basket of wood. "Can I say thanks for your help by chopping more wood for you?"

Sophie set the plate of bacon and eggs on the bench in front of him. "If you really want to, thanks." She nodded towards the window. "You can look at the view from there, or we can eat in the dining room. But I warn you, it's not as warm as in here."

Nate pulled out a wooden bar stool and sat. "Here's fine."

Sophie sat beside him with her plate and for a few minutes, food was the only thing on Nate's mind. Aside from a pink fairy cake last night, he hadn't eaten since yesterday's lunch. "This is a great breakfast, thanks."

She nodded. "About your car—"

"Is there a chance you could give me a ride back to Denby after I've chopped the wood?"

She frowned, and the sinking feeling returned to his stomach.

"About that, it's unfortunate timing. My car is in for repairs. I hit a roo down near Denby Crossing.

Hector—he's the town's only mechanic—gave me a ride home. He'll bring my car back in a couple of days, but—"

"So you're stuck here until then?"

"*We're* stuck, unless you want to try skiing cross country."

"A couple of days . . ." So much for his interview. So much for a skiing break after the interview. With fresh snowfall, the hotel had probably already given away his room when he'd failed to show up last night.

"Are you heading up to Storm King Lodge, or further?"

"I have—*had* a meeting at the lodge. Without a car and with no way to call them I guess that won't happen now." Frowning, he looked at the world beyond the window. White and unmarked yet by human or animal, it was serene and calm and very inviting. If he'd been looking at it through a window at the lodge, it would have been perfect.

But Sophie's home offered no distractions, no Internet, and no chance to let Spencer know he was definitely interested if a job was on the table. Would the company still be open to talking to him by the time he'd found his way to the lodge?

"You're lucky your car made it to my door. There's very little traffic on this road and the snow's probably set in for a few days."

He turned on the stool and faced Sophie. She was pretty, not in the conventional way perhaps, but morning light revealed delicate features and highlighted the sprinkling of freckles across her nose and cheeks. She'd been kind to a stranger and, he realised as he picked up both plates and carried them to the sink, being stuck on her farm shouldn't be seen as a hardship.

At least, not for me, he thought. "Very lucky. I half expected you to send me to the barn to sleep but you didn't, and that breakfast was great. I'll wash the dishes."

"No need, I'll do the washing up."

"Okay, then point me in the right direction and I'll start chopping wood. Bigger pieces for the fire in the lounge, smaller for the range, right?"

Sophie tipped her head and looked at him with surprise. "You sound like you know what you're talking about?"

"That was my job when I was in high school. My parents owned a farm. I'm a design engineer now, but I'm pretty good with mechanical stuff too. If there's machinery that needs fixing or tuning up, I'm your man."

A sparkle lit her eyes. "Let me think about it."

***

As Sophie dunked the plates and added detergent to the hot water, her mind reeled. An engineer? Would Nate have some ideas for how to make her project work? Could she be that lucky?

By the time she'd stacked the washing up on the dish drainer, the rhythmic sound of the axe biting into wood rang from the woodshed. Sophie dried her hands, put on her coat and boots, and slipped outside. From her favourite spot on the back veranda, she hunkered down beside Crackles and watched Nate swing the axe with an economy of movement and efficiency. She waited until he split the current piece of wood and set the axe in the chopping block, an old ironbark stump that had been there when Sophie bought the place, before she spoke. "For a city bloke, you've got style."

He set his hands on his hips, barely out of breath despite the pile of split wood around the stump. "I mentioned I chopped wood when I was younger. You don't forget old skills just because you're not using them every day." He began collecting the split pieces in his arms and stacking them under the eaves beside the house.

She looked at the height of the pile in surprise. He'd added two rows to the near end in the time she'd washed up and tidied the kitchen. "You don't have to cut me an entire winter's worth of wood, you know."

"I figure you burn a fair bit between the kitchen range and the open fire in the lounge." Nate removed the axe and hefted another round onto the block. "I'll do this lot—" he pointed to an untidy pile waiting to be chopped. "If you've got any other jobs, let me know what and where and consider them done."

Sophie took her gloves from her pocket and pulled them on then stepped off the veranda, intending to head to the barn and feed the chickens squawking for their breakfast. But Nate's offer to do *any* other job made her pause. "When you say you'll do *anything* . . ."

He grinned. "There is a caveat on that. I'll do it, so long as you have whatever tools or materials are needed. I could fix my alternator if I had a spare, but I don't. What do you need?"

"Can you make Santa Claus appear?"

##

"In July? Are you Santa's private secretary or something?"

"How do you know about . . . " Pink rushed into her cheeks, highlighting the freckles. She frowned and pinned him with a look that he knew carried a question—what had he been doing while she made coffee last night—but the question remained unasked.

Both his hands rose and he shook his head. "I swear I didn't mean to pry. I happened to notice a letter on your desk while I was trying to get a dial tone. That's all."

She twisted her hands together and looked away, out over the snowy paddocks and a stand of gum trees. Snow sparkled white and clean down the northern sides of the trees. "I don't know quite what I am, or why that letter was sent to me, but having received it, there's no way I'm not going to try to fulfil Jackson's wish for his little brother. So this letter I got . . ."

His thoughts flew back to the address on the envelope. "To Santa at the North Pole. Guess I missed the sign on your driveway." He looked around. "Where do you keep the reindeer?"

"I don't have . . . oh, forget it." She stomped away through the snow towards the shed.

Why did I say that?

It had seemed funny in his head but clearly Sophie didn't agree. He loosened the axe head from the stump. Women he liked, especially when they were as pretty as Sophie, disengaged his mouth from his brain. It was his biggest failing, and now he'd blown things with her.

He swung the axe and split the round into two pieces. As soon as Sophie reappeared, he'd apologise.

And then he'd find out why she needed Santa to appear. Clearly it had something to do with the letter to Santa, but as far as he could see, Sophie looked nothing like Mrs Claus, let alone the jolly fat man in the red suit.

Questions tumbled in his mind like clothes in the drier. Why had his comment touched a nerve? It was July, for heaven's sake.

And what did she mean by *appear*?

Chapter 4

Six still-warm eggs nestled in the cane basket as Sophie trod carefully across the snowy yard; Nate's jibe about reindeer was still bugging her. Stupid, she knew, but it had ripped open the wound left by her ex. Their break up was still fresh in her mind—was three months recent enough to be considered *fresh*—but she had to stop dwelling in the past and reach out to Jackson's family.

Putting her own problems aside, she needed to answer his request. Time seemed to be critical. How long did his brother have left? She had plenty more questions, but until she was reconnected to the outside world, that was all she had.

Questions, and an unexpected, unwanted guest.

She stopped at the corner of the garage, eyeing the way he swung the axe and buried it in the stump after he'd finished chopping the round. One hand rose and gripped the neck of her coat. So he knew how to chop wood and he wasn't some weird stalker guy, and maybe he was handsome, but the same reasons she'd left Denby, and Mark-cheating-Jones, and bought the farm still applied. Nate had just shown his true colours more quickly than her ex, and he triggered her discomfort meter to a bare notch below peak level.

Nate collected the fallen wood into a heaping armful and headed into the house. The screen door banged shut behind him, breaking Sophie's uncomfortable line of thought. He'd been pleasant and thoughtful until that crack about her and Santa.

Just like Mark. She'd thought he'd liked her idea to help sick children. His parting shot—delivered when she stumbled across him with Jenna Morton's body pressed hard against his in the cold room of the Denby supermarket—still stung. *You don't live in the real world, Sophie. Grow up and stop thinking you're Tinkerbell.*

Tinkerbell!

Get over it, Sophie, she chided herself. Gran had hugged her tightly when she'd shared the shattering discovery Mark had dumped her, and offered a simple home truth.

The right man is out there and he'll love you for being you, and everything you do.

Clearly that wouldn't be Nate Greenwood. Not that she wanted it to be him—heavens, she wasn't even thinking about looking for another relationship—but a little less sarcasm would make the rest of the day more bearable.

She crossed the yard and reached for the handle just as the screen door swung open.

Nate stood aside and held the door. Splinters of wood lay red against his cream cable-knit sweater, thicker over his left arm and chest where he'd held the load. Squashing an inexplicable urge to reach out and brush them off, she held the basket of eggs between them and stepped past him.

"Sophie." He followed her into the kitchen.

She set the eggs on the white-pine island bench and stood behind it, recognising the defensive position for what it was, but unable to change her reaction to this sort of conflict. "Thanks for bringing the wood in."

"I'll bring some in for the lounge fire too, but Sophie, I'm sorry about that Santa crack."

So not what she'd expected him to say. Her lips parted and she barely stopped the comment escaping.

Picking at a split end of cane on the basket, she pressed her lips together and thought for a moment before meeting his gaze. There it still was, that open, steady look in his eyes. "Why did you say it if you didn't mean it?"

"In my head it sounded funny. I'm sorry." He turned and headed towards the back door.

"Wait. Look, it's fine and—" She drew a deep breath. "I guess it was—*is* humorous when you don't know— I mean, a Santa letter in July sounds crazy. It's just that there's this little boy, Jackson. He wrote to Santa asking him to visit his little brother who's dying and—" Tears pricked her eyes.

"Oh God, I'm really sorry. I'd never have said what I did if I'd known, but why did you get the letter?"

She turned her head and sniffed. "I know the guy who works in the Denby post office. I'm pretty sure he sent it to me because he knows—"

Could she reveal her secret wish to a virtual stranger? It had ripped apart the fairy tale of her relationship with Mark, but was that a bad thing? Wasn't it better to be up front about the important stuff in life? Shoring up her nerve, she looked into Nate's eyes.

"You don't have to tell me, Sophie. It's none of my business. But I am sorry for upsetting you."

"You couldn't know why I reacted as I did.

Sorry about that by the way. I'm not usually such a snippy person. Besides, I'm not properly set up yet—" She drew a deep breath and gripped the egg basket. "And you wouldn't have guessed, even if the new sign had been at the gate, but I want to run my farm as a place where dreams come true for sick kids."

Nate barely missed a beat. She was willing to bet it was nothing like he'd expected to hear, and yet, his response was immediate. "That's terrific." He sounded sincere. There was even that little nod of his head and the crinkles around his eyes when he smiled at her.

Sophie blinked rapidly, her fingers tight on the handle of the basket. "It is? I mean, of course it is." She tipped her head to the side, curious to find out more about Nate who was suddenly so not like Mark. *So far.* She'd do well to keep a tight rein on her delight in that fact. "Why do you think it's terrific?"

"I can see you're passionate about the idea and being able to make a child's dream come true—that's special."

"Thank you." She looked away, unable to hold his grey-blue gaze. His open admiration was unexpected, tipping her off balance. If Nate meant what he said, was it possible she could actually ask for his help?

And then it happened . . .

"If there's anything I can do to help, tell me."

It wasn't as if she'd been holding her breath waiting for him to say it. She hadn't even been imagining herself willing the words into his mind. But his offer gave her the opening she needed. "Any chance you could tell me how to rig up something to make Santa and Rudolph fly in here?"

"Fly?" Frowning, he crossed to the window, leaned on the bench and looked out over the snowy ground. "You want to *fly—Santa and a reindeer* into your yard?"

When Nate said it, it sounded—huge. Crazy and impossible and what on earth was she thinking, but Sophie's heart sank. "I hate to disappoint Jackson and Ricky, but I get it; the task isn't possible—"

Nate shook his head and turned to her. "It's not *impossible*, but it depends on what you consider a reasonable compromise."

"Pardon?" Her disappointed brain struggled to get beyond Nate's '*it's not impossible.*' "You have an idea?"

***

"You don't need an *actual* sleigh driven by
176

Santa to fly in, do you? I mean, if we could create the illusion of Santa . . ." He caught the scent of vanilla and fresh hay as Sophie joined him and looked through the window.

"I guess if Ricky is only five, an illusion might work." There was a trace of disappointment tinged with doubt threading through her voice.

But Nate's mind was kicking into overdrive. "I thrive on challenge. Leave it with me. I'll take a walk around and get the lay of the land. How far does your property extend on this side?"

"Beyond the stand of snow gums, there's a post and wire fence. That's my eastern boundary. I'll have coffee and biscuits ready around eleven if you want morning tea."

"Thanks, I'll be back by then."

Nate brought in wood for the lounge fire, stacking the logs neatly in the stone alcove beside the fireplace, then collected his iPad from the car and set off towards Sophie's snow gums.

Weak winter sunlight broke through the clouds and glistened on the snow-covered eastern sides of the trees. They branched out wide and rose thirty metres— an appropriate height for the idea taking shape in his mind. But it was the splashes of orange, vibrant amidst the greys and browns of the bark that caught his eye.

He photographed the trees from several angles and checked the sight lines to Sophie's rear veranda before selecting the best tree for his concept. Finally, he made a video of the area with his observations as the soundtrack. When he played it back, the slow squeak-crunch of his boots breaking the crust of virgin snow came through loud and clear. Living and working in the city, he'd forgotten how much he loved such simple pleasures. He paused the playback and spent several minutes strolling around the majestic snow gums and listening to his passage. Frigid air stung his cheeks, his breath puffed white as he walked, and he felt more alive than he had in the past five years of city living.

"Na-ate?" Sophie's call brought him back to the present.

He glanced at this watch, surprised by how long he'd been lost in thought, and called, "Coming," then retraced his steps across the yard. He left his boots on the rack inside the back door and entered the kitchen. Sophie was setting slices of fruit cake on a serving plate along with two of the pink-iced fairy cakes. Two wooden kitchen chairs were drawn up in front of the range.

"Help yourself to coffee. I promise these are the last of the fairy cakes by the way. I'm working on my cooking repertoire for when I have special guests." She gestured towards the range and set the plate of cakes on the island bench where they could reach it without leaving the warmth from the stove.

"Will Jackson and his brother be your first guests?"

"If they accept my invitation, then yes."

Nate poured coffee into two mugs, carried them to the bench and set them down. Given the scope of projects he'd already designed, Sophie's request was relatively easy, but it excited him in a way he hadn't expected. He waited until she was seated before meeting Sophie's eyes. "I know how it can be done and I'd love to help set it up, if you'll let me?"

Chapter 5

Nate explaining his plan was a revelation. How she'd ever thought design work would be boring was beyond her, not when Nate's passion for it shone through every word.

No longer was he the unexpected, unwanted guest who made her feel awkward. Was that because she was over distrusting all men after her ex's betrayal? Or was it more about Nate himself? Nate, the good guy, the man who willingly offered his skills to help make a little boy's dream come true?

Pulling her wandering thoughts back to the present, she focused on Nate's plan. "So you'll rig a zipline from one of the snow gums to the back of the barn and it will carry the outline of a sleigh. I get that part."

"Then we project a video of Santa in his sleigh onto the blank screen and synchronize the timing of the animation with the flight of the screen along the zipline. From a reasonable distance such as your back veranda, the projection should look real. Santa will appear to land behind the shed then your actual Santa will come out of the front doors with his Santa sack and meet Ricky and Jackson. I'll double-check all the measurements, but it's very doable. What do you think?"

What did she think?

Sophie smiled, a huge half-moon kind of smile. She could feel it slipping across her face, pulling her lips up and stretching muscles she hadn't used in far too long. Probably her grin was too wide and she was about to gush her gratitude, but that didn't matter. Nate had solved her main problem in a single morning.

"It's brilliant!" Sophie clasped her hands beneath her chin. "I'll ask Hector to see if his father will play Santa for Ricky. Oh, Nate, I'm so excited I could kiss you—"

Heat rushed up her cheeks. She set her hands over the betraying colour and turned to the window. "I didn't mean . . . that just sounded weird."

Nate chuckled. "Definitely not weird when a beautiful woman says she wants to kiss you . . . but I get that you meant that in a non-real, I'm-so-happy kind of way."

"Absolutely." And there was that something else

besides her cooking skills that needed work before her first guests arrived. "I get a bit emotional at times. Before Ricky and his family arrive, I need to learn techniques to master my emotions. I can't wreck their special day by tearing up."

Nate nodded, drank the last of his coffee and stood. "On that note, is it okay if I explore in your shed and see what gear you've already got and and what we need to buy?"

"There're piles of boxes that I *inherited* when I bought the farm. Help yourself."

His gaze dipped to her lips. At least she thought that's where he looked before he turned abruptly and strode out of the kitchen. The idea that Nate might actually be thinking about kissing her—might actually want to kiss her—sent butterflies fluttering in her stomach.

He was only here for a day or two until the phone line was fixed or until her car was returned. He wasn't sticking around so even if he kissed her, what was the point? But now the thought of kissing Nate had taken root in Sophie's brain. She didn't want complications in her new life. Not even complications like kissing Nate.

***

Nate sorted through stacks of dust-coated boxes and antiquated gear that had come with Sophie's purchase of the farm. How anyone could have accumulated so much stuff in a single lifetime was beyond him. Unlike his mother, who culled clothes seasonally and spring-cleaned her home within an inch of its minimalist life, the previous owners must have been real hoarders.

He'd barely made it through the first layer of stacked boxes. The last two had contained mouse-nibbled magazines from the 1960s and 70s, and a pile of children's old story books.

As he lifted the next box, he spied a black metal steamer trunk. Old fashioned and dusty, with rusting metal corners, still, it looked more promising than the cardboard cartons he'd already sifted through. He dragged it into a clear space and tested the sturdy clasps. With resistant squeaks, they opened and he peered inside.

In place of the hoped-for tools he found more clothes from early in the previous century, dark fabrics made to last. He flipped up the top layer. A small section of cheery red material beckoned amid the dark clothing.

Nate dug deeper and pulled out a neatly folded pile of red with . . . was that white trim part of the red outfit?

Intrigued, he held one edge and shook the red and white outfit open. "Well, I'll be blowed."

"Someone must have played Santa here a long time ago." Nate spread the Santa outfit, complete with hat and wide black belt, over the kitchen chair. He wasn't sure why he felt compelled to show it to Sophie rather than tell her about it, but it seemed like a sign. Not that Nate believed in such things, but they *were* embarking on a Santa project. "Do you know anything about the previous owners?"

"Nothing other than their names. I've only met the neighbours on the eastern side once. The day I moved in they were clearing the cattlegrid at their front gate and I stopped to say hello. They invited me over for a meal and I put them off with a pretty pathetic excuse of needing to unpack."

Neighbours. Why hadn't he thought about that before?

"That's a shame. Do you know how far it is to their house?"

Sophie glanced through the window towards the

snow gums. "I'd guess maybe two kilometres, three at most? Why?"

He grinned at Sophie's frown. It seemed she'd been wrapped in her bubble of self-isolation until his car died at her front gate. "Maybe they'll have materials I can buy or borrow to set up the zipline."

"Good thought. So the only vaguely useful thing you found in the shed was the Santa suit? It's something, I guess."

"Didn't you look inside?"

"Not since I inspected the property. Unpacking my stuff has taken all my time and energy since I moved in last month. Exploring someone else's boxes just didn't matter."

"I get that. You look pretty well set up here now though?" Despite the old furniture, or perhaps because of it, he'd thought Sophie had lived here for much longer.

"I am, but back to my neighbours. Being without a car isn't a problem. We could ski cross-country."

"I was thinking the same thing. And maybe they'll have modern technology—like a sat phone."

Shrugging, she headed towards the wet room off the kitchen. A moment later she stuck her head around the door. "Well? Are you coming? It was your idea after

Chapter 6

Sophie followed Nate between the line of trees that formed part of the border between her farm and the Morgan's. A twinge of embarrassment grew into a cringe that tightened her stomach. Why hadn't she made some effort to get to know her nearest neighbours?

And now I'm about to call in only to ask a favour.

It felt wrong but, impelled by a sense of urgency to fulfil Jackson's request for his little brother, she told herself—hearing the words in Gran's voice—to get over herself.

They came out of the trees into a white landscape under a pale blue sky. Ahead of them lay an open, downward-sloping field blanketed in untrammelled snow. Reluctant to mar its pristine beauty, she stopped at the edge and called, "Nate!"

He turned back to her, his skis angled across the slope. "What's up?"

"Nothing. It's just—this field is beautiful, like a

scene on a Christmas card."

His gaze roamed the view and he nodded. "True."

The field glistened in its whiteness, with undertones of blue beneath the winter sun. Narrowing her eyes against the brightness, she looked into the distance. Stands of trees dotted the landscape and raised bare branches to the sky like soldiers on parade. "I've only skied cross-country higher up the mountain. I just wanted to take a moment to appreciate it all."

"I need to stop and appreciate where I am more too. I enjoy the challenge and the peace of cross-country skiing, but work has been full on for the past few years. I haven't had time for a holiday."

"Maybe you haven't made time. It depends how important something is to you." Having voiced that thought to Nate, realisation hit. Hadn't she done the same thing? Closing herself off from everyone had little to do with making time to unpack. It was about what she valued. Well, from now on, she was putting people first. "It might be time to re-evaluate things."

Nate seemed thoughtful, his gaze, unfocused as he turned towards the white field. "I love skiing, but it's been ages since I've made it to the snowfields. Hey, look!" He pointed with a ski pole.

Sophie followed the direction of his pole. A small herd of deer approached, stepping delicately through the snow. "I don't believe what I'm seeing. They're beautiful."

"Didn't you know your neighbours were farming deer?"

Much to her regret she'd begun to realise how little she knew of her new home and neighbours. "I guess I shut myself away to lick my wounds." Oops, she hadn't meant to let that slip out.

"What wounds, Sophie?" Of course, Nate didn't let it go. His voice was gentle, but his gaze said he wouldn't let her get away with fobbing him off. Not in this peaceful shared moment.

Huffing out white breath on the chilly air, their eyes met.

She shrugged. "I walked in on my ex in a clinch, with his tongue down the throat of one of my friends. Ex-friend now."

"Ouch. That's lousy, but hey, better to know sooner rather than later, right?"

Sophie pressed her lips together, keeping in a less than elegant snort. "True. I'm not sure if it was worse or better to stumble across them where I did."

"In your bedroom?"

"Nothing so stereotypical. They were making out in the cold room of the local supermarket."

"Seriously? That's —"

"Cool, in every sense of the word. They were caught on security camera and"— the snort she'd managed to contain erupted. Gulping air, Sophie let the humour roll through her for the first time since that day's hideous events—"she was dismissed for unhygienic food-handling practices."

It was Nate's turn to grin. "I was going to say weird, but *cool* fits."

Strangely, sharing that story and this moment with Nate didn't sting like she'd thought it would. Maybe she was moving forward, moving on, getting over Mark. Whatever it was, standing on the edge of a perfectly beautiful scene with Nate felt like standing at the beginning of something new. Like a fresh page waiting for the next chapter of her life.

He's leaving in a day or two. Maybe in a few hours if we find a working phone. Remember!

That didn't stop her gliding slowly towards him, her skis crunching through the snow crust. "But I couldn't face buying frozen products from that store again, and then one morning, I saw the ad in the real estate window and I bought the farm."

Nate turned his skis downhill without losing eye contact. "Something good came out of that freezer encounter then. In a roundabout way, you have your ex-boyfriend and ex-best friend to thank for where you are now. Following your dream." He pushed off and led the way down the slope towards the herd of deer. A long way beyond them, twin spirals of smoke rose above a line of bare branched trees.

Sophie watched Nate for several breathless moments before digging her poles into the snow and pushing forward, certain now that she wanted to kiss him. She wouldn't, but she wanted to.

Feeling gratitude because she'd been betrayed was all kinds of strange, totally left field thinking. And it was exactly what she needed to realise Mark no longer had the power to hurt her. Nate's words were the gift of release and empowerment.

Was her unexpected and unwanted guest her personal Santa in disguise?

***

Nate approached the Morgan's farmhouse with

an odd mixture of hope and a sense of impending loss. If Sophie's neighbours had the gear he needed to construct the zipline for Sophie, that would be great, and if they had a satellite phone so he could call a mechanic and then Tom Spencer—

Anticipation about leaving should have made him keen to get back on the road. Instead, it left him feeling conflicted. Arranging for delivery of a new alternator and explaining why he'd missed a meeting with his potential new employer meant his time with Sophie suddenly had an end date. In a day or so, maybe in a matter of hours, he'd have the means to leave.

And he had to leave; he knew that.

The short time he'd spent with her had reminded him of happier times, when work and deadlines and chasing awards that brought recognition for his work didn't dominate each day.

He had to go.

But he'd miss the chance of getting to know her.

The sound of Sophie's skis swishing alongside his as they skied towards a picket fence and a gate sheltered by a snow-covered shingle roof brought him back to the present. Analysing the reasons why he'd miss her after such a short acquaintance could wait.

191

He shook off the odd feeling and glided up to the gate, dug in his poles and bent down to unsnap his boots from his skis.

Beside him, Sophie did the same. "That was fun."

Her cheeks were pink and her eyes, bright, and her smile—how had he thought her simply attractive? She was beautiful, inside and out, with her plans to make a dying child's wish come true. Before he left, he'd make sure she had the means to make Santa and Rudolph fly.

***

Sophie knocked on the front door and stamped her feet to shake off some of the accumulated snow. A flutter like a flight of butterflies skimmed through her, but a little nervousness was good. It meant she was finally reconnecting with people. "Let's hope they're home."

"I hear footsteps." Nate's breath was warm across her cheek and she glanced at him, catching a hint of his cologne before the door was opened and her middle-aged neighbours' smiling faces appeared.

"Hi, sorry to drop in unannounced, but my phone isn't working."

Emma Morgan stood aside and ushered them in with a smile. "Don't be silly. It's lovely you've finally made it over here. Come in out of the cold. Welcome, Sophie and—"

It felt as though Nate had been around for more than a day, but Emma's rising intonation reminded her the Morgans hadn't met her guest. "This is Nate. Nate, meet Ernst and Emma Morgan."

Nate shook hands with her neighbours. "Great to meet you."

Ernst clapped a hand on Nate's shoulder. "I didn't realise we had a couple next door. When we saw Sophie the day she moved in, we thought she was single."

"I am single. I mean—"

"I'm a friend of Sophie's."

Their replies overlapped much to Ernst's confusion and Emma's amusement.

Sophie was a little taken aback. *Nate had dived in with that disclaimer pretty quickly.*

"Nate's just visiting and helping me with a project."

As if she'd needed another reminder not to dwell on the almost-maybe kiss, or imagine anything happening with him. But of course there *was* nothing between them. Nothing more than a shared desire to create a special early Christmas for one little boy.

Maybe there was something to her ex's claim. Maybe she did tend to filter life through rose-coloured glasses, imagining everything could be fixed with her brand of optimism. Pinning a neighbourly smile to her face, she took control of the conversation. "I'm sorry it's taken me so long to call in to meet you properly and I promise to do better next time, but this is more than just a social call. Nate's car died at my gate—"

"And Sophie has plans to give a dying boy a special early Christmas and we need some gear to make it happen."

The Morgans exchanged a look Sophie couldn't interpret, but Emma took Sophie's arm and drew her into the kitchen. "Ernst and I are happy to help in any way we can. While the men sort through Ernst's workshop, we'll put the kettle on. I've just taken a tray of Brownies out of the oven."

Chapter 7

Ernst's workshop exactly suited Nate's need for order and precision. Every tool was in its place on two long shadow boards, and a series of plastic boxes of varying sizes were neatly labelled and stacked one-or two-high on metal shelving. The only mess was wood shavings on the floor around a Triton workbench. A pair of safety glasses hung off the end of a piece of timber waiting to be fed into the machine. Ernst must have been working on it when they knocked at the door.

"This is my kind of shed." Nate glanced up. Various lengths of timber lay across beams with cargo netting stretched beneath.

"When you live as far from the nearest hardware store as we do, it's good to have frequently used materials on hand. Tell me what you need."

Nate pulled his phone from his pocket and opened the note he'd sent from his iPad. "I'm setting up a zipline to fly Santa and his sleigh in. One of Sophie's snow gums is the right height and angle to set up the starting point. I'll take the line across to the back of her shed. The idea is for someone dressed as Santa to then appear from the shed."

"You?"

Nate shook his head. "I won't be here, but Sophie mentioned Hector's father?"

Ernst nodded. "From Denby. Long way to come to play Santa, but Joe does it every Christmas for the kids in the Crossing. Who's the child you're doing this for?"

Nate struggled to remember the surname. "Ricky something."

"Milton." Ernst's expression darkened. "That family has had the worst run of luck I've ever seen. And now you say their youngest is dying?" He shook his head. "Poor buggers. Anything I can do to help, just say the word."

Half an hour and one almost-full container of tools and gear later, Emma appeared in the doorway. "If you two have gathered what Nate needs, coffee's ready."

"Coming, darling." Ernst caught his wife around the waist and pulled her in for a quick kiss. He kept his arm around her waist as they headed down the hallway.

As Nate followed them through the house to a

more modern kitchen than Sophie's, he felt something shifting inside him. The Morgans behaved like his parents used to, back before his father's diagnosis and the illness that had led to his loss of mobility and a move into the city. Dad spent his days permanently confined in a wheelchair in a low-set suburban house that his mother had made a home. Their farm had been sold to finance the move.

Because I didn't want to give up my dream of becoming an engineer to become a farmer.

His parents had loved the farm. It must have broken his father's heart to give up the home that had been in his family for several generations, but they'd done it rather than pressuring Nate to change his mind.

An ache began building in his chest. Guilt over his decision? His selfish choice? His parents had never reproached him for it; they'd wholeheartedly supported his dream. He pressed a fist over the ache and knuckled the area until it eased.

Maybe the ache was a sign telling him it was time to do more than just live his dream? Now it was his turn to make someone else's dream come true. This time it was for Ricky.

And Sophie.

Emma handed him a mug of coffee and a plate with a still-warm Brownie giving off a mouth-watering smell. "Did Ernst have everything you needed?"

Drawing on the good manners instilled in him by both his parents, Nate shook off the odd sensation and smiled. "And then some."

Ernst picked up his Brownie but delayed popping it in his mouth to speak. "Glad we had most of what you needed. Shame about the lack of phone service given what happened to your car, but at least we can contribute materials for your project. I'll bring them over in the ute when we've finished here. You'll be able to get started this afternoon."

Sophie seemed surprised. "Contribute? Oh, but I fully intend to pay you for—"

Ernst held up one hand. "Not happening, Sophie. This is our small contribution to making that little boy's last Christmas special."

Nate felt a lump in his throat and, when he glanced her way, Sophie's eyes were glistening.

She blinked several times before responding. "Thank you."

##

Nate stood beneath the snow gums and

rechecked his measurements before he began construction of the zipline. He was happy—revelling in the chance to actually make what he'd designed. Opportunities to do hands-on stuff were rare and he'd missed working with tools and materials, feeling rough wood take on the shape and smooth texture of his design.

But this could be no more than a hobby. Engineering steel structures for the Spencer Company would be a wonderful challenge, one he was keen to explore. After all, they were headhunting him and he was happy to take the next step in his career.

But as he began sorting through the timber looking for the thick hardwood piece to bolt in the beginning of the zipline, he realised this happiness he felt now was different to what he'd felt when he'd been offered his first graduate job. That feeling had been tied in to the fact his work would be close enough to visit Mum and Dad on the farm every weekend—before Dad had lost mobility. The move to Spencer's firm would change that. Their head offices were in Sydney; his parents were now in Coffs Harbour enjoying the relaxed coastal lifestyle. Weekend visits would become more difficult, especially in the first couple of years when longer hours and a high rate of output would be expected.

Enough. Time to think about that later. He set up the ladder, attached his tool belt, also borrowed from Ernst, and set his foot on the first rung. For now, he planned to concentrate on the task at hand and really enjoy bringing his vision to life.

Maybe he'd come back for a visit on the day Sophie hosted Ricky and Jackson and their family. It would great to see if his flying Santa could bring a smile to their faces.

***

Sophie stood on the rear veranda beside Nate, her hands deep in her jacket pockets. The afternoon was well advanced, but a shaft of sunlight touched the snow gums, making the white and orange bark vibrant against the darker background. The zipline was barely visible. She took a deep breath of cold air tangy with the scent of winter foliage and smoke. "I can't believe you've finished rigging it up already. This is so exciting."

"I'll have to start it manually for now, but you'll be able to set Santa flying using a remote control on the day."

Nate tramped through the snow and climbed the

ladder into the branches of the snow gum. His voice carried clear on the chilly air. "Ready?"

"Yep, ready."

An outline of Santa and his sleigh floated out from the snow gum's branches, flew across the yard and almost touched down before it disappeared behind the barn.

Nate returned to her side, his grin, infectious. "How was that?"

"It's great. Now we just need the image to fit on the outline."

Nate picked up his iPad and opened a file. "I've been having a play with a few of my videos."

"You keep videos of *Santa* on your iPad?"

His laugh was wry. "Probably not what you think. They're from last Christmas when my cousin and her young daughter were visiting from Melbourne." Nate handed her his iPad and tapped the screen. "I think this one works well. It will give you some idea how Santa will appear."

A lifelike video of Santa in his sleigh flew across from the left side of the screen, growing larger as it reached the right hand side and disappeared.

"That's what the outline will look like once I've

rigged up the projector. What do you think?"

How to express her joy? "When you suggested creating an illusion, I felt kind of let down, like I wasn't giving Jackson what he wished for his brother. But this flying Santa video combined with a real Santa coming out of the barn—" She flung her arms wide and hugged Nate. "Thank you!"

This close, with her nose buried in his cream jumper, the smell of damp wool combined with scents of fresh-cut wood and something citrusy that must be his cologne. All very appealing when they came in a neat Nate-shaped package that included intelligence and passion. So very appealing . . .

Nate gently eased her arms from his neck and stepped back, creating space between them. He met her eyes, but his smile had dimmed, replaced by an expression she couldn't interpret. "You're welcome, Sophie. I'll ferret around in your storage shed and see if I can find a Santa sack to go with the outfit I found this morning." He took the three steps off the veranda like a cork popped out of a bottle of Champagne.

Heat exploded, rushing up her neck, filling her cheeks and blowing away her composure. An apology flew from her lips. "Sorry about that—hug."

He stopped and, half-turning his head, spoke over his shoulder. "It's fine. No big deal."

"I didn't mean anything by it. I'm just excited." She turned away and grabbed the basket of kindling she'd been taking to the kitchen when Nate stopped her to show her the zipline in action.

"Not a problem. I'll be in the shed if you need me."

"Dinner will be ready in an hour."

She stepped through the doorway, the screen door closed behind her and she huffed out a sigh of embarrassment. Such stilted conversation felt wrong after the wonderful day they'd had. Wrong, and disappointing when they were creating something so special.

Oh Lord, why had she hugged him?

***

Nate lifted an armful of musty clothing from the trunk and dumped it on top of two unopened cardboard boxes then stood looking at nothing. What was his problem?

Sophie had simply hugged him to express her thanks and delight. It didn't mean anything more than that. How could it when they'd only met a day ago? So

203

why had he stepped away like a scalded cat?

Forget it, he told himself. You'll be gone tomorrow.

That damned ache started up in his chest again. He stood straight and dragged in a series of choppy breaths. Was it a warning of heart problems? He was only thirty, but his grandfather had dropped dead of a heart attack at forty-five, long before Nate had been born. He pulled out his phone to Google 'signs of a heart attack', tried to open a browser then stared at the screen.

Right, no service. If he had a heart attack there'd be no chance of help.

Pressing a hand over the ache, he made his way back to the house. Back to Sophie and warmth and—

The moment he entered the kitchen and saw her stirring a pot at the stove, the ache eased.

She lifted the pot off the range and turned, giving a short yelp when she saw him leaning against the doorjamb. "Sorry, I didn't hear you come in." She frowned, put the pot down on the island bench and took a couple of steps towards him. "Are you okay? You look . . ."

Her voice trailed off and he closed the gap between them. "I'm not sure. My chest hurt, here." He set his hand back where the pain had been.

She frowned at the spot where his hand lay. "In your heart?"

Chapter 8

"I know I can give you an aspirin if you think you're having a heart attack." Sophie's hand rose and her fingertips settled lightly above Nate's hand while, with her free hand, she checked his pulse. His heart beat firmly in a regular pattern and his pulse was steady, unlike her uncle's the day he'd had his first attack. "Sit down. Your heartbeat feels normal. Does your chest still hurt?"

Nate's gaze met and held hers as she gently pushed him onto a chair. He frowned, shook his head, then moved his hand until it covered hers, pressing it flat over his heart. "No. It was there and now the ache has gone."

"So the pain was—there exactly?"

"Yes."

In her mind, she sorted through her first aid lessons, learned after her uncle's heart attack. "Were you exerting yourself? Lifting heavy boxes, anything?" What other questions had the paramedic asked about her uncle's condition as he talked to her on the phone? He'd told her to administer an aspirin. The ambulance had been fifteen minutes away and she fully believed her uncle's life had been saved by the instructions she'd received in that phone conversation.

"I was standing, just looking at a pile of clothing."

"Any pains elsewhere, like in your arms, neck, jaw? Any nausea? Light-headedness?" Were there more questions she should ask? But Nate's pulse continued steady beneath her fingers and his colour was good. Nothing like Uncle Terry's grey pallor.

Nate shook his head. "None of those."

"I'm no expert, but I don't think it was a heart attack. Maybe it's something less sinister, like a panic attack. I'll ski over to Ernst and Emma's place and get him to pick you up and take you to—"

He caught her wrist preventing her from moving away. "Don't leave me, Sophie. I feel—better with you here."

"Are you sure you don't want me to get Ernst?"

"I'm fine." His thumb brushed across her hand, which still rested over his heart. "I was thinking about a decision I have to make when the ache started. I think you're right. I didn't realise just how much of my life will change depending on what I choose."

"Sounds pretty important. Do you think the fact you're stuck here with me and unable to do anything about your decision might have made it worse? Is it time sensitive?" That was her concern about the Santa project for Ricky. She had no idea how much or how little time he had left.

"That meeting I mentioned I was going to? It's about a new job, and a pretty big step up for me if I take it."

Keep him talking. Maybe you can help him work out what's worrying him. "Are congratulations in order?"

"Maybe. Yes. I don't know. I'm still thinking about it and what it will mean. But I don't know if the offer will still be on the table. I missed the interview and I haven't been able to make contact to apologise or explain."

"Surely they'll be understanding when they hear what happened. I mean, things happen, right? That's life."

Nate's arrival had come right when she needed practical help. Being able to answer Jackson Milton's request and make his wish for his little brother come true was the first good thing that had happened in months, if she didn't count finding Wishfort Farm. But that had been for her, and it had only been possible thanks to her trust fund. Turning twenty-eight had its compensations.

Somehow, Sophie realised her hand was stroking Nate's cheek. Short stubble felt soft beneath her fingers and it was impossible to stop. She'd always liked clean-shaven—until now. But Nate's stubble defined his jaw in a very appealing way.

He leaned closer and his lips brushed hers in the softest of kisses. It felt natural to kiss him back. Natural and as necessary as her next breath. The clean, fresh scent of snow gum and chopped wood, snow and something that was uniquely Nate surrounded her. It was all new and exciting, and yet—it was like coming home.

When she finally raised her head, she was short of breath and halfway to lost in Nate. She'd never felt so alive.

And it scared her silly.

***

Nate lay awake long into the night. Thoughts about the job offer were jumbled in with worries about his parents and, intruding on both were those kisses with

Sophie.

He didn't regret kissing her, not one bit. He wanted to repeat and expand the whole wonderful experience, so why had he run from her hug? Sure, it had taken him by surprise, but there'd been nothing more than gratitude in it. Besides, he wouldn't be here much longer. A few more hours, a day . . .

When he got mobile reception, he'd be able to explain to Tom Spencer why he'd missed that meeting, and tell him—tell him what? That he would be taking the position? He waited for his chest to tighten.

Nothing.

Maybe that ache in his chest had been a panic attack after all?

If Sophie was right, wouldn't the thought of whatever was causing such an attack trigger another one? If it wasn't about the new job . . . logic told him to follow the line of thinking further.

He thought about his parents. On his last visit, they'd been happy, the happiest he'd seen them in several years. Dad had joined a lawn bowls team and was involved in a mentoring scheme for retirees. He loved helping teenagers in woodworking and metalworking classes.

Lucky kids. All the times he'd spent in Dad's work shed learning how to craft useful and beautiful timber items with Dad were now precious memories.

And Mum's constant anxiety over Dad had vanished beneath a more friendship-focused life. Between her glass-working classes, her book club, and Dad's renewed interest in working wood, Nate could make a pretty good guess what he'd be getting next Christmas. Folding his hands behind his head, he chuckled.

But if work and family life hadn't triggered another ache in his chest, what was left? Personal life?

He had friends, good mates and colleagues with whom he partied on Friday nights and fished on weekends. There'd been a few girlfriends—he could count them on the fingers of one hand—but no special woman who made his heart zing or who had inspired thoughts of forever.

Tipping his head to look through the window, he caught a glimpse of the late-rising moon. Sophie must have a similar view from her room along the hall. Tomorrow night she'd be looking at it alone.

It hit him then, an ache that was like a giant black hole in his heart. The idea of not being around

Sophie set his heart thumping, as though it wanted to jump out of his chest and hide so he never had to leave.

One day. That's all I've known her for. It's crazy to imagine she's the reason.

But that little voice in his head knocked the idea of *only one day* out of the ballpark. His parents had known they'd found their special someone after a single date and married within two months.

For a long time, Nate lay awake staring at the moon.

Chapter 9

Sophie stoked the embers in the range then added two small pieces of wood. When they caught and flames danced along the edges, she closed the metal plate and moved a large frying pan onto the hottest spot.

Her eyes felt gritty and her mind leapt from one thing to another without settling on anything. Tossing and turning through the night because Nate's kiss played and replayed in her mind was out of all proportion. Two nights Nate had been here—*two nights*—and yet, his kiss had felt so right. Like coming home.

But the kiss hadn't meant anything. Not to Nate. He'd been anxious about the pain in his chest and her explanation had reassured him. That's why he'd kissed her. Neither of them had mentioned it later or made a move to repeat it.

It was important that she didn't allow that kiss to colour their morning. With any luck, the phone line would be repaired and her car would be returned today. She just had to get through this morning without embarrassing herself by mentioning it and then Nate would be gone.

One thing that kiss had shown her though—*this will be the last time I think about it*, she promised herself—she was over Mark. Well and truly. The kiss had happened and she'd enjoyed it because she liked Nate. He was helping make her first *When You Wish* project come to life. Why wouldn't she like him?

She dropped rashers of bacon into the pan and stabbed them with the corner of the egg flip. *I bet Nate slept well. Bet he didn't think anything more about kissing me.*

"Good morning."

She spun around at the sound of Nate's husky voice. "Morning." He was neatly dressed, but when she met his eyes, shadows darkened them. "Did you sleep well?"

"The bed's very comfortable. Can I help with breakfast?"

"Sure. If you want toast, pop some bread in the toaster." She added three eggs to the pan. They sizzled alongside the bacon. "Breakfast won't be long."

Minutes later, with bacon and eggs plated and coffee poured, they sat side by side at the bench beneath the window. "Looks like we had more snow last night." She knew when it had started falling, having lain awake into the wee hours.

"It started around midnight."

He knew?

"You were awake then? I thought you said the bed's comfortable?"

Nate set his cutlery down and half-turned on his seat, his gaze intense. "It is, but something kept me awake."

Concern jagged in her stomach. "Were you in pain again? Maybe I did the wrong thing when I called it an anxiety attack? I can ski over to—"

"I'm fine, in the health department at least. No, I was thinking about what you said and trying to figure out what might be causing the tightness in my chest."

Sucking in a breath because her chest had grown tight too, she assessed his face. Aside from a slight puffiness under his eyes that mirrored her own, his colour looked good. *He* looked good, as though he belonged there. It wasn't going to be the same without him at her kitchen bench. "And did you? Figure it out I mean."

Nate nodded. "I did. It's you."

Sophie dropped her knife. It clattered onto the china plate while her grip on her fork tightened. "What do you mean? Is this about me hugging you? I said I was sorry and I meant it."

"I'm not—sorry that is. I'm glad. It made me realise something my mother and father believe to this day. I know my arrival here happened because of a failing alternator—that's a fact—but think about it. I completely missed the Morgan's driveway and found yours. My engine died right in front of your house."

"I'd call that good luck in the fog that night."

"Normally, so would I. But sometimes the way things happen seems like more than good luck. Under normal circumstances we probably would never have met."

"Please don't tell me you believe in fate."

He smiled. "No. But I do believe that, sometimes, life lands us right where we need to be in that moment. I was so certain that I'd accept the job offer at that meeting I missed, but after I kissed you, I started thinking about why I'd felt that tightness in my chest."

"You were worrying about the job?"

"I thought that at first, but it wasn't that. When I

kissed you—it was like coming home. And when I thought about not being around you, the ache returned."

Coming home? Did the echo of her words mean something, anything? Or was she projecting her response onto Nate?

"Why are you shaking your head, Sophie? I thought you felt it too?"

"I did—I do. But Nate, it's not possible. How can we feel like that? Seriously! We've known each other less than two days. In fact, we don't really know each other. I don't know anything about you and—"

He set a finger over her lips. "There's a simple way to test it. Kiss me, right now."

"You're crazy." But there was nothing she wanted to do more. Leaning towards him, he met her halfway, his lips gentle, tasting of coffee and bacon. She kissed him without dwelling on how short a time it had been since he'd landed on her doorstep. She kissed him without worrying about what her family would say if they knew. She kissed him because there was no way she could *not* kiss him and live another moment.

She lost herself in Nate's kiss—which led to thoughts of other things, like coming home to him every day of her life. Things she'd never truly imagined with her ex. Shoving the wisp of thought aside, she wrapped her arms around Nate's neck and simply *enjoyed.*

The insistent trill of a ringing phone broke through their bubble. She stared at Nate for a moment. "The line must be fixed."

Sophie rushed down the hallway with Nate close behind, and grabbed the phone. Cupping the handset, an exuberant "Hello" burst from her lips. Listening intently, she smiled and nodded at Nate. "That's great news." She offered him a thumbs up signal.

One of Nate's eyebrows rose and there was a question in his eyes.

Covering the mouthpiece, she said, "It's Hector, my mechanic in Denby. Do you want me to ask him to bring up an alternator for you?"

"Yes please." He gave her details of the make and model of his car to tell the mechanic and waited until her conversation ended.

She set the phone in its cradle. "Hector was letting me know he'll be bringing my car back late this afternoon. He doesn't have an alternator in stock, but he said he could arrange for one to be delivered and bring it when he comes with my car. Is that okay?"

"Perfect." He glanced at the phone and frowned.

"Would you mind if I made a call? I need to get in touch about that meeting I missed and see if the company is still intending to offer me that job."

"It's all yours. I'll be in the kitchen, reheating breakfast." With a smile, she left him to make his call.

But as she warmed their plates, her heart grew heavy. They had the morning to enjoy whatever this attraction between them was before Nate fixed his car and left. Hours, minutes, and then he'd have to go.

Would she see him again or would he realise his great job offer was the most important thing, not pursuing a relationship that started and ended with a kiss?

No matter how totally right it felt, or how crazy it seemed, maybe meeting Nate was meant to be. Not for romance, but to remind her to follow her dream.

If only that dream included Nate.

Chapter 10

Nate wiped his hands on a rag, folded it to a cleaner patch then wiped the oil cap. On the other side of his car, Hector's young apprentice mechanic tightened a nut.

Hector checked the work then looked at Nate. "That should do it. Start her up and we'll see how we did."

Nate slid into the driver's seat and turned the key in the ignition. The motor purred. On the dashboard display, all the lights glowed, but his GPS screen still showed a broad swathe of green and no roads. He turned the engine off and climbed out. "The engine sounds great. Thanks for your help."

"No problem. It's more efficient to fix your engine here than to leave a part with you only to discover another problem later and then have to drive out again. Sometimes a battery needs changing after the alternator goes; not often, but it can happen."

"All fixed?" Sophie picked her way through the

snow, stopping beside the open bonnet and peering in.

"I'm good to go." Nate gave his business card to Hector. "Thanks again. Send me your invoice and I'll transfer payment to your account when I'm back in mobile range."

"Will do. I'll tell Dad about the Milton boys and your Santa plan too. Give him a call when you have a date. See you, Sophie."

Nate closed the bonnet and stood beside Sophie watching as Hector's work truck drove off with the apprentice at the wheel. Tyre marks from the truck and Sophie's car, a neat blue Rav 4 now parked in her garage, had churned the snow to slush. "I guess I should get on the road too."

"Would you like to stay for dinner? I've got a lasagne that only needs reheating." Her smile stretched a little wider than usual.

He wanted to stay, but what was the point of delaying his departure? It wasn't like one more hour would make leaving Sophie any easier. "Tom Spencer offered to meet with me over breakfast in the morning, so I really need to get up to the lodge tonight."

"Okay. Well—" Her expression seemed disappointed, kind of how he was feeling.

He couldn't just climb in his car and drive away. "A cup of coffee would be very welcome before I go."

"Of course." Sophie turned quickly and walked towards the open front gate.

Nate stowed his overnight bag in the boot and strapped his skis on the roof rack, then joined her at the kitchen window and stood looking at the view.

"Nate, I can't thank you enough for your help with the zipline idea. Would you—I mean, there's no obligation to—but if you wanted to come out and meet the Miltons—"

"I'd love to, thanks. I wanted to ask if you minded, but I wasn't sure if that was a bit pushy."

"Not at all. It's going to happen thanks to your brilliant work. I'll let you know the date once Jen Milton gets back to me. I called them while you and Hector were fixing your car." Her glance slid away. Through the window, dusk gathered in grey shadows and black silhouettes. "Ricky only has a few weeks."

Nate set his empty coffee mug down and touched her elbow. "It must be hard for them, but what you're doing—it's a beautiful thing."

"I want to help them make special memories they can remember and relive after Ricky has gone.

Making good memories helps those left behind, knowing their precious child got to do what they really wanted to." She sniffed softly. "I have to work on not getting emotional on the day."

"True. Try to focus on what you just told me; how you're helping them create memories. You're the provider of experiences and the maker of wonders. Enjoy that, and the joy you'll see on the kids' faces."

"I will, and thanks for that reminder."

He slid his hands around her waist. "Sophie, I really don't want this to be goodbye, but I have to be at this interview tomorrow."

She nodded, but didn't meet his gaze. "I know. This is your career and it's really important." Her hand cupped his cheek and she rose on tiptoes and kissed him softly.

It felt like goodbye.

When she finally looked up her eyes glistened. "I'll always be grateful you came into my life when I needed a push in the right direction. Thank you for helping me to realise my dream."

An hour or so later, Nate turned onto the road leading to the lodge. Banks of packed snow rose a good two metres high on both sides of the narrow cleared road. The skiing would be great and he was determined to fit in a couple of days on the slopes. If the job offer was made and he accepted, who knew how long it might be before he'd be able to take another break?

But as he pulled up in front of the lodge, he was less sure than before about taking the job. It was far away from Sophie and yes, he knew it was crazy, but he was just like his parents, because he knew Sophie was special; he wanted time to show her that, and for them to get to know one another.

He picked up his phone from the dashboard holder, noticing it had three bars of reception. The lodge used a satellite dish to maintain connection with the outside world. If Sophie had a small one, she could easily operate her new business online without worrying about the landline going down.

If Sophie had a satellite dish. The idea opened up other possibilities that might help his situation too.

Heading towards the reception desk and still thinking about where to position a dish on her roof, he didn't see the man until he heard his name.

"Nate Greenwood? It is you, isn't it? Tom Spencer." Spencer held out his hand and shook Nate's.

"I'm heading to the bar. Care to join me for a nightcap?"

"I'll check in first, but, sure." He had no more time to think about what he wanted. Spencer would likely want an answer tonight, but Nate still hadn't worked out his next step.

The only thing he was sure about was that he wanted a chance to get to know Sophie. His parents weren't the only ones who knew straightaway that they'd met *the one*.

Nate stopped abruptly in the middle of the hallway leading to the lounge bar and a couple bumped into him. He turned, offered them a quick "Sorry," and stepped to one side. What was happening to him? He'd jumped from 'getting to know' Sophie to . . .

Waiting for what his mates described as *the stomach clench* at the thought of being tied down, instead he felt a sense of excitement and rightness. He'd just thought *the one* in relation to Sophie and the cringe factor he'd felt whenever his parents told the story of their first meeting hadn't happened. Sophie wasn't beside him, but the thought of a future with her made him feel great.

"Nate, over here." Spencer's voice cut through the noise of the bar and Nate's realisation. He moved

past a group standing around a tall bar table and joined
the man whose job offer he was about to reject.

Chapter 11

Jackson and Ricky Milton and their parents, Jen and Jace, sat around the small outdoor table Sophie had decorated with kid-friendly Christmas treats: gingerbread men, candy canes, and a plate of iced Christmas tree cookies, thanks to Emma Morgan lending her cookie cutters for the occasion.

Sophie set down her tray and handed around mugs of hot chocolate and marshmallows, pink and white and plentiful. "Your snowman looks like he'd enjoy a marshmallow or two. What do you think, Ricky?"

Smaller than the average five-year-old and pale-skinned from months in and out of hospital, Ricky was a smiler. The disease that was stealing his young life day by day hadn't diminished his ability to enjoy treats. He took two pink marshmallows from the bowl then hesitated and looked at Sophie. "Can I have one now and another one with my drink please?"

Sophie glanced at Jen, who nodded. "Sure, help

yourself."

Ricky took a third sweet and popped it into his mouth. His smile lit up his whole face.

"Come on, Ricky. Let's feed the snowman." Jackson held out a hand and the two brothers walked over to the lopsided snowman, laughing aloud as they tried to push soft marshmallows into the snowy head.

Jen pressed her lips together and sniffed. "This is such a lovely outing for the boys, thank you so much, Sophie."

"It's my pleasure. We have one more special treat I hope they'll enjoy too." The *ding-dong* of the doorbell interrupted further conversation. "Excuse me. I won't be long."

Hurrying down the hall, she prayed it was Hector's father in his Santa suit. He was late, and the Miltons couldn't stay much longer.

She pulled open the door, her prayer momentarily forgotten as she drank in the sight. "Nate, you made it." It was impossible to stop from wrapping her arms around his neck and pulling his head down for a quick kiss.

He touched his forehead to hers. "Sorry I'm late. I had to pick up a little surprise from Ernst and Emma, but I wasn't going to miss meeting Jackson and Ricky, and seeing Santa's arrival out of your barn."

"Oh, don't remind me." She gripped his shoulders and peered around him, frowning at the empty steps and yard, and the silence beyond her gate.

"What? Don't tell me I missed it?" Nate frowned.

"No, it hasn't happened and the Miltons will be leaving soon. Hector's dad hasn't arrived." Her heart twisted as though it would burst from her chest in despair. "My first effort at fulfilling a special wish and I've failed—big time."

"Have you called him?"

"He confirmed he'd be here when I checked this morning. I can't think why he isn't here."

Nate appeared thoughtful. "I have an idea. Is the projector all set up and ready to go?"

"Yes, but without Santa, it won't be the same."

"Do you have the Santa sack handy?"

"Yes." She slipped into the lounge and came back holding a brightly-coloured Christmas sack bulging with presents donated by locals who had heard of her plan for Ricky's Christmas celebrations. So many people wanted to help—she had far more presents than one child would ever need—so Sophie accepted donations with the proviso they could be used for any children in need of Christmas cheer.

Nate took the sack and tucked a strand of hair behind her ear. "Give me ten minutes then start the projection. Santa will be there. Believe, Sophie." He bounded down the front steps and disappeared down the side of the house.

Sophie set an alarm on her phone then made her way back to the little family enjoying hot chocolate on her back veranda. Pinning a smile on her face, she joined the adult Miltons and sipped her hot chocolate.

Her phone pinged a reminder when ten minutes was up. Crossing her fingers, she stood and asked the boys to join them on the veranda. Holding her phone up, she wiggled it and grinned. "I received an important message that a very special visitor is on his way. Who do you think it might be?"

Jackson stared at her. "Is it—Santa?" He looked so eager and yet unsure that she nodded and then winked. He took Ricky's hand and turned to look out over her yard. "Who do you want to see, Ricky? Close your eyes and make a wish."

With complete trust in his big brother, Ricky

closed his eyes. "I want to see Santa—and Rudolph."

Sophie's heart thudded. Rudolph she couldn't supply, but Nate—she trusted him. Below the edge of the table, she pressed the button and activated the projector and sound system.

Across the snowy yard, a faint jingling of sleigh bells carried on the clear, cold air, growing louder and nearer and—

"Look, Ricky, it's Santa!" One arm around his brother's shoulders, Jackson pointed towards the snow gums, now barely visible in the fading light. Flying through the air came a sleigh drawn by eight galloping reindeer and leading them, a small, red-nosed Rudolph.

Ricky jumped up and down, calling, "Hello, Santa, hello!"

The sleigh disappeared behind the barn and, moments later, the barn door opened. Out stepped Santa with a bulging sack of presents. And behind him on a short lead and stepping daintily, came a small, shy deer with a nose that glowed.

"Oh my. How—?" Jen Milton covered her mouth with both hands and tears ran freely down her cheeks.

Sophie stared in wonder. She'd guessed that

Nate intended to put on the old Santa suit, but where had Rudolph come from?

Santa strode towards them and stopped at the bottom of the steps. "Merry Christmas, children. And Merry Christmas to your parents."

Ricky reached out towards Santa. "Are you really here, Santa?"

Santa dropped to one knee and held out his hand. "I'm really here, Ricky. Your brother wrote a wonderful letter to me at the North Pole, and my friend Sophie arranged for you to come here to see me. You see, it's summer where I live, but the reindeer love snow, especially Rudi. Would you like to meet Rudolph? He said he knows he's your favourite of all the reindeer, but don't tell the others!"

Ricky and Jackson moved slowly forward, Jackson still with his arm around his brother.

"Hold your hands out, like this, and let Rudi sniff you first."

The boys did as Santa told them and approached slowly, hands held out. The deer licked Ricky's hand and he giggled.

Tears filled Sophie's eyes. Blinking to clear them, she swiped both hands over her damp cheeks and breathed through her mouth.

Santa patted Ricky's shoulder and chatted quietly to him before delving into his sack and pulling out the first of several presents, including one special one for his brother.

Jackson unwrapped the present and held it out for his parents to see before turning back to Santa. "Wow, my own camera. Thanks, Santa!"

Santa glanced at Sophie, but spoke to Jackson. "You could ask Sophie to take some photos of us. I think she might know how to use a camera."

Jackson held out the camera. "Please, Sophie?"

"Of course."

Santa put an arm around Ricky, and handed Rudolph's lead to Jackson. "Smile, everyone. Say cheese for Sophie."

And in that moment, as she captured precious memories for Jackson and his parents of the night Santa and Rudolph flew in to visit Ricky, Sophie knew Nate was her *one*.

Epilogue

24 December – five months later.

Nate climbed down the ladder and stepped back to survey his work. It had been hot under the summer sun, but the new satellite dish was in place on Sophie's roof. She'd be thrilled to have her Make a Wish website up and running before Christmas, but he hadn't felt so nervous, even at his first interview, as he did about the rest of the day. Not that the satellite dish made him nervous.

He touched the box in his pocket for reassurance. Everything would be fine.

The only sadness had been news from the Miltons that Ricky had passed away peacefully in his sleep three days ago, his precious Rudolph toy tucked under his arm and his family around him. They had a hard road ahead of them, but Nate felt grateful that they'd been able to share one final, special Christmas together—all thanks to his big-hearted, wonderful Sophie.

"Nate? I've poured you a cold drink." Sophie appeared around the corner of the house, a short summer dress swirling around her thighs as she walked towards him. "Come into the shade and relax."

"Says she who's been online all morning with her newly connected website, making plans to make more children's wishes come true. How about you relax with me?"

"There's one sure way to make me—"

He caught her around the waist and pulled her close. "Hmm, I wonder what that might be?"

She walked her fingers up his chest, pausing at the bump in his shirt pocket. "What's this?"

"I'll tell you later—*after* you've relaxed."

She arched an eyebrow at him. "Is it my Christmas present?"

"Depends. Are you on Santa's naughty or nice list?"

"I don't know, but you'll be in his good books for the next few Christmases after filling in for him last July." She sighed. "This one will be really hard for Jackson and his mum and dad."

"We were able to give them one more very precious Christmas with Ricky, thanks to you. You're a very special woman and—" He tugged her towards his car. "Come on. I can't wait to give you one of your gifts."

They drove along the dirt tracks to Sophie's gate and Nate stopped a little short. He came around and opened her door. "Close your eyes and don't open them until I tell you to."

"I'm not sure about closing my eyes."

"Trust me, you'll be glad you did."

Guiding her with an arm around her waist and holding her other hand, he led her through the gate and turned her towards the first of his gifts. "Okay, now open them."

***

When-U-Wish Farm

Where dreams come true.

The sign was everything she could have hoped for and then some. "Oh, Nate, it's beautiful."

Warmth bloomed somewhere in the region of her heart as the perfection of the sign Nate had painted for her sank in. Slipping her arm around his waist, she blinked away tears and met his gaze.

"Do you really like it?"

"Absolutely. You've caught exactly what I want

this place to be. This is about believing in your dreams and making them happen." She rose on tiptoes and kissed him. "Thank you, my darling. You've made my dreams come true. I hope yours do too. Did Tom Spencer accept your offer to keep working for him if he let you telecommute now we have the satellite dish?"

"He went for it, which is a relief since I rejected his first offer." Suddenly Nate looked rather nervous. He reached into his shirt pocket and pulled out a midnight-blue velvet box.

He opened it and her heart wanted to leap out of her body, for inside nestled an antique diamond and ruby ring, the one she'd admired in a store window on their weekend away.

"You've helped me find another dream I never expected, but one I'm hoping will come true. Sophie, you are my special *one*. Will you marry me?"

Struggling to speak around a lump of joy, she nodded, sniffed, and held out her left hand. "Maybe the other dream wasn't yours alone, but mine as well. Yes, Nate Greenwood, I'll marry you."

"I love you, Sophie Denby, giver of dreams."

The End

Thank you for reading. If you enjoyed this story, please consider leaving a review on Goodreads and/or the retailer from whom you purchased this book.

<u>Acknowledgements</u>:

With many thanks to my wonderful friend, my editor, Annie Seaton.

Short and Sweet: 4

Follow the Sun

ANNIE SEATON

Dedication

This book is dedicated to those who have lost, grieved, and learned to heal.

Acknowledgements

A big thank you to my editors and proof-readers: Roby Aiken, Susanne Bellamy, Anna Welch and Kristen Woolgar.

A special thank you to Heather Stuart for letting me use Feath's Mobile Coffee in my little story.

242

Chapter 1

Misty

Monday

Dawn lifted the darkness silently like a blanket being gently removed from a sleeping world. Misty O'Farrell held her camera as a faint tinge of pink edged the indigo sky. She waited patiently, and the pale hues deepened to apricot, and the first glimmers of gold heralded the rising sun. Towards the horizon, a line of white froth broke the flat silver of the sea as a boat headed out to the fishing grounds.

Misty let out a soft sigh and blinked back a tear as the top edge of the sun peeked over the horizon. She didn't let herself cry anymore. A new day, another new beginning.

Tears didn't help. Crying did not ease grief; beginning each day with a positive attitude and then creating her art helped her. She shivered and pulled her mohair cardigan more tightly around her chest. The chill was increasing by the day as autumn took hold. It was time to follow the sun and keep heading north.

Misty waited until the orb was half visible and pressed the shutter, taking the one single shot she allowed herself each day. The sand began to shimmer in the early daylight as the tide flowed over it. Rising to her tiptoes and holding her camera against her chest, she leaned over the railing of the lookout, watching as the last of her work from yesterday washed away.

Beautiful Snapper Bay was edged by a scythe of shimmering sand and when the last circle of yesterday's work disappeared in the gentle surge, Misty turned away and headed back towards her campervan. It was parked on the grass at the edge of the headland half a kilometre away. She'd left Harry asleep in the back, and he'd be getting restless if she didn't get back soon.

'Good morning.' Misty nodded and smiled

as she walked past the group of men sitting at the wooden table under the shelter adjacent to the lookout. They'd been there each of the five mornings she had watched her sunrise in this coastal village; it was about time she was friendly.

'Morning, love.' The older man with the grey beard lifted his hand in a leisurely wave, but the other three men only stared at her curiously and didn't return her greeting. Each of them held a large coffee mug. One of the biggest thermos flasks she had ever seen sat in the middle of the table.

'Another lovely day in paradise,' she replied.

'Sure is.' The bearded man nodded and turned back to his friends. Four sets of binoculars also sat on the scarred table and she wondered what they were looking for. Whatever it was hadn't appeared, because they had been there every day since she had arrived.

Okay, if you don't ask, you don't find out anything local.

Misty stopped and turned back towards

them. 'May I ask what are you looking for?'

Four sets of eyes were on her. To her surprise, it was one of the other men who answered.

'Mullet.'

'Mullet? As in the fish?' She stepped closer to the table.

'Well, most of us are past the haircut—not enough hair these days—although Bobby here had a beauty back in the seventies,' the same man said.

'A haircut?' Misty pulled a quizzical face. 'Oh, you mean a mullet haircut!'

'Told you she was a strange one. Not very quick on the uptake.' The thin man at the far end of the table scowled at her.

'Jocko, be nice.'

Jocko shook his head. 'Nope. I won't be to someone who free camps at our beach. Plenty of good caravan parks here trying to make ends meet.'

She stared back at him and took note of his red aura. 'I am a bit slow on the uptake this time of the morning.' She kept her voice friendly and even. 'Once I get a coffee I'll be sparking on all sixes.'

'Sheesh, that says it all,' he persisted. 'It's sparking on all fours, you dimwit.'

She ignored the persistent rudeness and kept her smile in place. The other three men were harder to read but at least they weren't being nasty.

'Okay, firing on all fours it is then. You know, I like to learn something new every day. There's so much we have to learn. Isn't it wonderful?'

Misty bit back a smile as the rude man stared at her and shook his head. 'Bloody hippy chick,' he muttered.

'So tell me about the mullet,' she said. 'Why do you need binoculars to see them? Can't you just go fishing? I saw one big boat go out.'

'Full of questions, aren't you, missy?' Jocko let out a rude snort. 'Why don't ya go back to your city and leave us in peace and quiet?'

'It's Misty, not Missy.'

'Welcome, Misty. Just ignore Jocko, he's a rude bugger. He likes the sound of his own voice.' The man with the beard interrupted. 'I'm Alex, and these two rough-looking heads are Ken and Bobby.'

'Nice to meet you all. Can I sit with you for a while and you can tell me how you look for the mullet?'

Alex and Bobby moved along the wooden bench seat to make room for her and Alex gestured for her to sit down.

Jocko glared, snatched up his binoculars and strode off to the lookout platform where she'd taken her photo.

Misty had taken a sunrise photograph there every day since she'd left home. Structure and ritual kept her sane. The chronicle of her three-year journey was a daily photograph of the sunrise and her sand art, wherever she was.

She slid onto the seat, lifted the strap of her camera over her head and placed it carefully on the table.

'Professional photographer?' Alex asked.

She shook her head. 'No, just an amateur learning slowly. So, tell me about this mullet?'

Alex nodded. 'The "mullet run" is what it's

known as. Happens up here every April, maybe May if they're late. With this crazy weather lately, we have no idea when they're going to run. Or even if they will run.'

'The mackerel didn't come last summer,' Ken said with a frown.

'Global warming?' Misty asked. 'And why is it called the run?'

'Well, you see,' Alex gestured to the beach, 'the sea mullet live in the estuaries and waters along the ocean beaches on the east coast. When they spawn, they head out of the rivers to the sea and "run" up the east coast. We keep an eye out from the lookout here, but most of the professional fishos will be down on the beach. It's a bit of a race to see who spots them first each year.'

'In the old days when we were down there, we played fair,' Bobby said.

'What do you mean "played fair"?

He shrugged. 'Mobile phones, bloody Facebook and all those other things. Half the time the world knows where the fish are before the fishermen on the beach get a whiff of them.'

'Do they wait in utes with crates on the back?' she asked. 'I saw some camped down there yesterday.'

'Yeah, those bastards. They come from the south and muscle in on our locals' catch.'

'Gets interesting. I've seen them come to blows over the years. Net rage,' Bobby said.

'It sounds interesting.'

'You go down to the beach every day, don't you, Misty?' Alex asked. 'We've seen you down there at low tide.'

She nodded. 'I do. At low tide.'

'Keep an eye out. When the mullet arrives you'll see a flurry of activity on North Beach when they put the nets out. Keep away from them, because they won't appreciate you getting in the road.'

'Specially with that stupid stick,' came an angry voice from behind her. Jocko was back and his face was red now. 'There's a couple of shadows in front of south beach. I think they're here, boys.'

Alex pulled his phone out and the other two men jumped up. 'I'll give Nugget a call. He's up at the top lookout.'

'Thanks for explaining to me,' Misty said, but the attention of the four men had shifted. 'See you later.'

She picked up her camera, looped the strap around her wrist and walked to the edge of the grass.

As she went to walk across the car park and head up the hill, a silver Audi purred past her. The driver parked it at the side of the road near the table, and her gaze lingered on the good-looking man who climbed out and leaned his back against the door.

'Come on, Angus. You almost missed it,' Jocko called out as he hurried back to the lookout.

Misty crossed the road and picked up her pace as she heard Harry kicking up a racket.

Oh no, he's awake.

Chapter 2

Angus

Monday

'You almost missed it.'

Angus McDonald closed the car door and drew a deep breath. He knew Jocko wasn't talking about the sunrise, but that had been his intention this morning. He'd given no thought to the mullet run stakeout.

The sun was already way above the horizon and the old fellas had left their table and crowded onto the lookout. The mullet must be on the move.

Just the morning he needed peace and quiet, and time to compose himself for a couple of difficult meetings ahead.

One work, one personal.

Slipping his keys into his pocket, Angus

watched a young woman crossing the road. When she reached the footpath at the bottom of the hill that led up to the headland past the four towering Norfolk pines, she paused and put her head to the side as if listening. Her blonde ponytail swished as she broke into a run. He looked ahead to see if there was something wrong.

If someone needed help?

There was nothing to be seen and he let out a breath with relief. The last thing Angus wanted was to get involved in someone else's dramas this morning. He'd had enough of that before he'd left home, and in the time it had taken to calm Sean down, he'd missed the sunrise.

'Bloody hero!'

Angus had ducked as a cup of hot tea whistled past his head and smashed against the living room wall. Brown tea had trickled down the pink wallpaper that no one had changed since Mum had died ten years ago.

Dad had been too involved in his fishing to care, and Sean hadn't cared about anything after the accident. Angus had been too busy trying to earn a living and keep Sean on the straight and narrow to worry about the house.

'Just piss off. Leave me in peace,' his brother yelled. Sean's voice was husky and his eyes were red-rimmed. It was obvious he'd been on the grog again last night. 'If it wasn't for you, Mr Perfect, I wouldn't be here, and I wouldn't have to put up with this!' Sean pushed himself out of the wheelchair and shoved it hard. Pieces of plaster flew into the air as the chair bounced off the wall near the door and the wheelchair turned on its side, one wheel spinning wildly as Sean hopped into the kitchen.

Angus had turned his back and picked up his car keys without a word. There was no point in speaking to Sean. He could get dressed for the office when he came back from the lookout. With a bit of luck, Sean would be out to it by then. There was no point talking or trying to reason with him when he was in one of his black moods, and a hangover only made him worse.

Now taking his attention away from the woman running up the hill, Angus reached into his pocket for his keys and clicked the remote to lock his car before strolling over to the lookout.

In the distance, above the heads of the four men who had kept him sane for the past three years, the sea was a brilliant blue, and the sky was clear. It was shaping up to be a fine day.

'What did I almost miss, Jock?'

'The mullet. Look!' Jock pointed to the north and Angus followed his gaze. Five utes loaded with empty crates were parked side by side at the beach just past the creek.

Angus frowned. 'Not locals?'

'No,' Alex replied quietly. 'So we'll stay up here. We're past the days of getting into a stoush.'

'I'll give Ron a call when I get to the office.'

'Appreciated. He'll take more notice of you and hopefully check their licences.' He gestured for Angus to follow him to the fence adjacent to the back of the lookout platform.

When they were out of earshot of the other

men, Alex turned his attention to Angus. 'How's Sean today? He was at the club until late last night. Our poker game finished at ten and he was settled in.'

'Not good. Chucked a cup of tea at me, and smashed the wall with his wheelchair.' Angus ran a hand through his short hair. 'Honestly, Alex, I'm at my wits' end. I don't know what else I can do.'

'It's not up to you, Angus. Sean's thirty. He's old enough to take responsibility for his actions. If he'd done that three years ago he wouldn't be in this position, and you wouldn't still be in this town.'

'But he didn't and I am, so I have to make the best of it.'

Alex grunted and shook his head. 'You're as bad as he is in your own way.'

'What?'

'Maybe if you left him to fend for himself, he might take a bit of responsibility. And you could focus on your career and stop working that second job so you can support him.'

Angus's gaze was wary. 'What second job?'

'Half the town knows you sneak out at night and clean the club after it closes.'

Angus closed his eyes. 'Half the town?'

'Well, a couple of us do. Jocko spotted you one night when he was walking home. If you didn't provide for Sean, he might apply for the disability pension.'

'His pride won't let him.'

'And your actions make sure of that. Son, listen to me. You're not doing yourself or him any favours. Promise me you'll think about it.'

Angus stared at his elderly friend. Alex had been his dad's fishing mate, and had been there for him ready to lend an ear since his parents had passed within a year of each other.

But he didn't know best this time. Angus knew where his responsibility lay. 'Thanks, Alex, I'll give it some thought,' he said to keep his friend happy. 'I'd better head for work. Big day ahead.' He tucked his fingers into the pockets of his hoodie. 'That wind's cold.'

'Grab yourself a coffee. The van's up at the top headland.'

'Feath's Mobile Coffee?'

'Yep, she filled the thermos for us at six.'

'She knows where the customers are this time of day.'

Alex grinned. 'She does, the lovely lass. Jocko went down when she set up, to tell those bloody poachers she's up here.'

'He went down there and talked to them?'

'He did. He's got a soft spot for Feath.'

'Was that the only reason? You lot aren't up to anything, are you?'

'Us? Never.' Alex's wide-eyed innocence had Angus frowning.

'Just don't go getting yourselves into trouble. The last thing I need is to go to court to bail you lot out of a fix.'

Alex patted his shoulder. 'We'd never do anything wrong. Trust us.'

Angus stared at him before he walked back to his car. 'I'll hold you to that.'

Chapter 3

'I'm coming. I'm back,' Misty called as she ran the last twenty metres to the van. 'Settle down, young Harry.'

She pulled the key from the deep pocket of the cardigan she'd knitted last winter. Being on the south coast of Victoria had been a shock to her system. She'd knitted two scarves, a beanie, and this warm fluffy cardigan from wool that she'd bought from a local spinner near Port Fairy. Apparently, the local fleece was an award winner, and Misty was beginning to appreciate its warmth as the weather turned cool. Cooler than she imagined the north coast of New South Wales would be.

She slid the door of the van open and a sad little face greeted her. She reached out and tickled Harry under the chin.

'Did I go without you, little man?' She climbed in and left the door open. Harry lay on his back on her bed as she tickled his tummy. 'It was too cold for you out there and your delicate little paws would have got wet. I hope you didn't disturb anyone up here with that naughty yapping.'

Misty continued to chat to the little white spoodle as she reached for his food bowl. Harry was a cross between an English Cocker Spaniel and a Toy Poodle, and he was unerringly loyal. He knew when she was feeling down, and he'd climb into her lap and gaze up at her until she snapped herself out of it.

'We're going to have a good day today. What will we draw today? I'm in the mood for pyramids.'

The dry kibble clattered into the bowl and Harry's attention moved to his breakfast. Misty pulled a face. 'My love's abandoned me for a bowl of dry dog food. And here was I thinking you were lonely.'

As she leaned over to put the kibble in the

side pocket of the van, she spotted another van parked on top of the hill. Misty leaned forward and smiled.

A coffee van.

'Stay here, Harry.' She grabbed a handful of coins from the console between the seats and climbed out of the van. Harry didn't even notice she was leaving.

Misty's nose twitched as she walked up the grassy hill to the crest where the coffee van was parked. It was a Lion's park, and technically she shouldn't be staying here, but no one had come and asked her to move. Which she would do if she was chipped.

The aromatic fragrance of freshly-brewed coffee drifted across to her. She looked down the hill to the beach behind her. There was a much better view from here. The tide had turned and was running out. It would be about three hours until low tide, so she could do some journaling before she headed down to the sand. The only worry was those utes and the possibility of getting in their way.

Maybe she'd have to walk right up the beach and find another flat bed of sand.

The van with the logo Feath's Mobile Coffee on the side was parked at the top of the park next to a couple of covered tables. Two men waited as their coffee was being made by a pretty young woman. Misty stood back and smiled at the heart-shaped sign that listed the coffees available.

When it was her turn she stepped forward. 'Good morning, Feath?'

'Yes, that's me, love. What can I get for you?'

'I'll have a chai latte, and I shouldn't but your muffins smell irresistible. Which would you recommend?'

'Sweet or savoury?'

'Go the savoury.'

Misty jumped as a voice came from behind her.

'Feath's cheese and bacon muffins are incredible.'

She turned and was surprised to see it was

the Audi man. Empathy flooded through her as she sensed the unhappiness that rolled off him; it was so strong she had to resist taking a step back, but she smiled and nodded. 'I can smell them so I think you may be right. I'll have two, please. Breakfast and lunch.'

'Coming right up,' Feath said. 'Your usual, Angus?'

His deep voice sent a shiver through Misty. 'The usual, thanks, Feath. It's handy you being here today. It means I don't have to drive out to the highway. You've saved me fifteen minutes there and back.'

'My pleasure. Besides,'—Misty smiled as Feath winked at the man called Angus—'the custom from the beach has been non-stop since six. I'll head out to the highway about eight-thirty and catch the nine o'clock commuters.'

'You're on the ball, that's for sure.' Angus turned to Misty. 'You've picked the best coffee stop in town. Just passing through or here to stay?'

His eyes were the most beautiful blue, not

pale and not dark; they were almost the colour of the parti-sapphire ring her mum had left her. Fringed by long dark lashes, Misty found it hard to look away. A shiver ran down her spine; she hadn't felt like that since . . . well since, before.

She returned his gaze steadily and decided it wasn't his unusual eye colour, it was the expression in them that had her mesmerised. 'Um, just passing through. On my way north.'

'For the winter?' His eyes held hers, and a curl of warmth unfurled in her tummy.

No.

'Maybe.' She shrugged. 'Maybe for longer.'

'Not on a schedule?'

'No. I'm a free agent.'

'Half your luck.' He stepped back as Feath held out her coffee and a brown paper bag. 'One chai latte and two muffins. Nine dollars, thank you, lovely.'

Misty put the coins on the counter and took her coffee and muffins. 'Thank you. And good luck with your coffee van.'

'Thank you, lovely. I'll be here tomorrow if you're still around. Zucchini muffins next.' Feath tapped the side of her nose. 'And if the mullet arrive, I'll be here all week.'

'If the mullet arrive,' Angus said.

'They will.'

'Still ever the optimist, Feath.'

Misty looked from one to the other as the conversation bounced along.

'Only way to be, love. Life's too short to be negative, and you never know what's around the corner.' She handed Angus two coffees and Misty watched as she put two muffins in the bag. 'I put one in for Sean too.'

'Thanks. You're a sweetheart,' Angus said as he handed over a twenty dollar note.

Misty realised that she was standing there when she'd been served, and had no reason to be listening to their conversation. Heat ran up her neck and she lowered her head and started off down the hill.

'Want some company?' came the attractive

deep voice from behind her.

She paused and looked up into those blue eyes. 'I haven't got far to go.'

'Nevertheless, I'll be a gentleman and see you get there safely. I haven't got far to go either.'

Chapter 4

There was no conversation as Misty and Angus walked down the hill together, but it was an easy silence.

As they reached the old campervan parked under a Norfolk Island pine tree, Angus juggled the cardboard holder with the two coffees and the bag of muffins into one hand. He held the other hand out to her. 'I don't think we've been formally introduced yet. I'm Angus McDonald.'

She removed her hand from her pocket and shook his. 'Misty O'Farrell.' Her breath caught as a tingle heated her hand. She half-expected to hear a crackle and see sparks.

He stared at her and suspicion laced his voice. 'There was no need to do that. I'm perfectly safe you know. Totally trustworthy, I can assure you.'

Misty stared at him with her mouth half-open, trying to process what happened. 'Do what?'

'That alarm thing.'

'What alarm thing?'

'The one in your hand.'

She uncurled her fingers and held up her palm. 'There's nothing in my hand.'

He frowned at her, but his expression was more surprised than irritated. 'How did you do that then? My hand is still burning.'

Horror filled Misty. He'd felt it too? That had never happened before. She'd been trying to send him some happy feelings, but she'd never experienced the heat that had sparked when she'd slipped her hand into his.

Her words stumbled out. 'It must have been the way I gripped your hand. I must have pinched a nerve. I'm so sorry.'

He was still frowning as their eyes met and held. 'That's okay. I'm sorry I jumped to conclusions. That was rude of me.'

He stood there for a moment staring at her, as though he, too, found it hard to break the connection. Because Misty knew there was a connection.

I'm not ready for this.

I won't ever be.

Unease built in her chest and rose to her throat, making it difficult to breathe as she was caught in his blue gaze. His aura was a soft orange, but she'd known instinctively he was thoughtful and considerate. With great difficulty, she dragged her eyes away and gripped her coffee tightly. 'It was nice to meet you. You have a good day, Angus.'

'You too.'

When she looked up again, he was striding down the hill to where his car was parked. He was a tall man. His shoulders were broad and, to her distress, her eyes settled on his strong thighs and well-filled jeans. She didn't look away until he rounded the corner and was out of sight.

Maybe it was time to leave this little coastal village. She usually stayed a month or so at each stop, and the five days she'd been here had flown. Contentment had settled over her since she'd arrived and she knew this was a good place to be. And the beach was perfect for her art. The park was perfect up here on the hill, and having her own tiny shower and toilet in the back of the old Coaster van meant she didn't need to go anywhere else.

Misty opened the door and let Harry out before making her way over to the bench seat at the edge of the cliff. Her stomach was churning with guilt. There was no way she could have felt like that. She didn't want to be attracted to anyone. There was no place in her life, or heart, for that.

She put the coffee on the bench seat beside her and stared north along the beach but didn't see anything. Gradually she became aware of Harry trying to scramble up into her lap. She picked him up and when he was settled she reached for the lukewarm coffee. Her appetite had fled; she would leave the muffin for dinner tonight.

'That was a very silly thing I did, Harry. I almost let someone in. You and I both know, I will never, ever, ever do that again.'

Misty looked north again, and this time she

took notice of what was happening. There seemed to be a lot of activity on the beach. Utes were reversing back and forth, men in wellington boots were strung out in a line along the edge of the water, and as she watched, they walked in waist-deep and pulled at something. Her eyes narrowed as she began to see the dark shape that was forming an oval in the waves. Suddenly the activity on the beach became almost frantic and as she watched, three men pulled a net in and then there was a myriad of silver fish flapping on the expanse of glistening sand.

Draining the last of her coffee, she put Harry on the ground and lifted her hand to shade her eyes.

'I think it's time we went to the beach.'

***

Angus

There had been no sign of Sean when Angus went back to the house; he had a quick shower and dressed for work. He left the second coffee on the bench next to the microwave, knowing that Sean would look for it when he surfaced. There were some things he could trust his brother to do.

The streets were still quiet as he drove the short distance from their house to town. The school rush—if it could be called a rush in their sleepy little town—hadn't started yet. The only children he passed were those waiting at the bus stop to catch the bus to the private schools.

Angus knew that trip well. To his father's dismay, he'd insisted on going to the senior college in Ballina. He'd known from an early age that he wanted to go to uni. Do something that would make a difference in people's lives, and not spend his days smelling like fish and stinky bait and spending his autumn waiting for the mullet run to begin. Dad had been disappointed, but at least Sean had gone into the family fishing business.

Now, the boats sat in the backyard of the family house. Kikuyu grew up through the wheels of the trailers, and the fishing nets rotted in the sun. If Sean would listen to him and have a prosthetic leg fitted, he'd be quite capable of running the business.

Angus huffed a sigh as he parked on the rooftop car park next to his office and made his way to the back door of the building. Despite the time that had passed, he imagined his hand was still tingling, and he ignored it. But he couldn't get Misty's face out of his mind. Her features were delicate and accentuated by the way she'd pulled her hair back, but her face held a gentle beauty.

His hand paused as he put the key in the lock.

Gentle beauty? Where the heck had that come from? He sounded like he was reading poetry, like those Shakespearean sonnets he'd studied for the HSC.

Shaking his head, Angus pushed the door open, preparing to face the day with a clear mind; he would ignore any thoughts of that beautiful woman.

'Morning, Angus.' Joanne, the front desk receptionist, was already at her desk. 'Coffee's brewing in the machine.'

'Morning, Jo, and thank you. I need another

one.'

'Up to see the sunrise again?'

'No, I missed it but the old fellas were there. The mullet run's starting, I think.'

'Hope so. The town needs a bit of a lift. A good season will see some money around.'

'We can only hope.' Angus turned towards the kitchen and paused. 'What time's Mrs Ryan coming in?'

'She's your first appointment at nine.' Joanne sounded apologetic. 'Sorry, she insisted.'

'No matter. At least it will be done and dusted early.'

Joanne gestured to the kitchen. 'I put two shots of coffee in the machine for you.'

Angus filled the largest mug with the strong coffee and headed for his office. As he crossed the room to his desk, his mobile buzzed in his pocket. He frowned. Not many people had his personal number, and he worried that Sean needed him.

He put his coffee on the desk and pulled his phone out. Glancing down at the screen showed an unfamiliar number. Early in the day for a scam call; they usually came at noon and six, but he didn't want to risk missing something important.

'Good morning, this is Angus McDonald.'

There was no reply, and he was about to disconnect as a quiet, hesitant voice spoke.

'Angus, it's Becky. Becky Barber.'

Angus tensed and closed his eyes. 'Becky, it's been a long time.'

Chapter 5

Misty

Tuesday

'Good morning, Misty.'

Misty smiled as she approached the table at the lookout. She could just make out Alex, Bobby and Ken in the light from the LED that Bobby wore on his head. There was no sign of Jock this morning.

'Good morning, gentlemen. You're very early today.'

'As are you, dear lady,' Ken answered. 'And your companion.'

'I was hoping that you'd be here,' she said. 'I want to ask a favour.'

'What can we do for you?' Alex asked.

'I was hoping I could tie Harry to the leg of

the table, and leave him here while I take my photo. Feath is setting up and there's already a coffee queue up at the park. I didn't want him to disturb her customers with his yapping.' She lifted Harry so that he could be seen in the dim light.

Dawn was still a way off. She'd been surprised to see the coffee van set up so early, but when the queue of men in work clothes and fishing boots began to snake along the path, she knew Feath was about to have a good start to the day. She'd call up after her photo and say good morning to the pleasant young woman, and tell her how delicious the muffins had been.

'Gentlemen, this is Harry. He'll be a good boy and I can promise he'll sit there quietly. He's used to me and my sunrise ritual.'

'No need to put him on the cold concrete, love,' Alex said. 'Give him here. He can sit on my lap.'

'It is a bit chilly this morning.' Misty smiled and handed Harry over. 'Thank you.'

Alex lifted a mug and passed it to her.

'Feath filled the thermos for us and she gave me a mug for you too.'

'Oh, how kind.'

'She said as long as you can drink the brew we do. Said you were a chai latte lady.'

'I'm a strong coffee lady at this time of the morning. Thank you.'

Ken and Bobby patted Harry as Alex unscrewed the cap of the thermos and the aroma of strong coffee reached Misty.

'Sit down for five. You've got a good twenty minutes before sunrise.' Alex handed Harry over to Bobby when he held his arms open.

'Yes. I wasn't sure if you'd be here, or if you'd want Harry. I didn't want to leave him up there. He woke up when I did, and he cries if I leave him once he's awake.'

'As bad as a kid,' Ken said. 'I remember our boys were like that. Judy couldn't leave the room without them squawking when they were little. Now we hardly see them. They live in Western Australia.' He chuckled. 'She reckons they all went west to get away from their cranky father.'

'They all went to the mines though, didn't they?' Alex commented. 'They'll come home one day. Everyone comes home to Snapper Bay.'

Misty found it hard to speak as her ever-present grief threatened to rise. Her throat was tight and her voice was thick. 'It is a special place. I've been made very . . . very welcome wherever I've gone.' As she lifted her camera, headlights cut a swathe in the darkness. 'Thank you. Be back soon.'

Their kindness was her undoing. Tomorrow maybe she'd take her photo from the Lion's park lookout.

The light from the headlights lit her way to the timber platform of the lookout. She'd known it was Angus before he'd even parked the car. Somehow she'd sensed him.

Don't be silly. He came yesterday so it was a natural assumption to make.

Cut the crap, girl, she told herself.

Misty stared out over the ocean as her heart thudded hard. Her body was not listening to her emotional commands. Dawn was creeping in, and the water was ruffled as a brisk breeze raced across the surface. It was only a minute before the wind swooped up the cliff and she wrapped her cardigan around her as the damp chill engulfed her. Tomorrow she'd wear her beanie. Reaching up, she slipped the scrunchie off her hair and let her ponytail loose so her hair covered her ears and neck.

The platform shook as someone stepped onto it behind her and she tensed.

'Good morning, Misty,' Angus said quietly.

'Good morning, Angus.' She forced herself to look up. In the growing light, she could see the dark shadows beneath his eyes.

He stepped closer and held out the coffee she'd left on the table. 'Alex asked me to bring this over to you. He said to take your time. Your pup is being spoiled.'

'They're a lovely group. Jocko wasn't there today though?'

Angus nodded as she took the warm mug and wrapped her hands around it.

'They are. And Jocko's down on the nets. They're all retired fishos. They were good mates with my dad.'

'Were?'

'Yes, we lost Mum and Dad a few years back. Mum had cancer and I still say Dad died of a broken heart.'

'Sad for you.'

'I started coming here a few years back to catch up with the fellas some mornings, and it's become a daily habit for me. Then it turned into watching the sunrise every day. A great way to start the day before I go to work.'

'What do you do? You're not a fisherman?'

He chuckled and the warmth of the happy sound lifted her heart. She visualised the last fragments of her sadness leaving with the breeze that had now moved on.

'Heck no. I'm the local solicitor.' Suddenly, the warmth left his voice. 'Not where I thought I'd end up, but we can't control what life does to us.'

'Does to you?'

'A long story for a rainy night.'

***

Angus

Angus almost added, 'Perhaps I'll tell you one night,' but he bit his tongue before he could say it. He didn't need any more complications in his life. Besides, Misty would move on soon. He'd seen it over and over through the years. Couples, singles, grey nomies, they came to town, enjoyed the surroundings, stocked up and moved on to the next coastal village. They'd follow the sun north for the winter.

Angus fought back the jealousy. Such a free life with no commitment to responsibility. He could live that way for a year or ten.

'You'd like to travel the road too?'

He looked at her, surprised that she'd almost read his thoughts.

'I think it would be a wonderful way to live, but my responsibilities don't allow it.'

She was quiet for a moment, and when she looked up at him, her eyes were sad. 'So many of us get caught in the trap of doing what's expected of us, we let opportunities go.'

A tinge of irritation crept in. What did she know of responsibility? Travelling in a beat-up old Coaster van with a dog for company, not working and doing what she wanted, when she wanted.

His voice was short. 'Have you finished your coffee? I'll take your mug back and leave you in peace to take your photo.'

'Don't you want to watch the sunrise?'

He did, but Angus was feeling cross with himself, and strangely, also with Misty because of the jealousy niggling at him.

'I do, but I can see it from over there just as well.'

'Please don't go. It's nice to have company.' She drained her coffee and put the mug on the railing at the side of the lookout and then switched on her camera.

Angus hesitated and then decided to stay.

They could be quiet and just enjoy the moment.

He took a deep breath as the edge of the clouds above the horizon took on a golden lining. A perfect balanced formation of cumulonimbus clouds sat above the horizon and, as the rising sun lit them from beneath, the clouds turned a soft pink.

The silence between Misty and Angus became comfortable, and he heard her draw in a deep breath too. As the sun split the horizon a shaft of golden light reared to the heavens in one of the most spectacular sights he had ever witnessed at sunrise.

Calm stole over him and all thoughts of Sean, his work, and this unwanted attraction left him.

Strangely, Becky Barber came into his thoughts, and he knew in the calm of that moment there was a solution to all his problems.

If only.

Chapter 6

Misty

Wednesday

'Hello, lovely.' Feath propped her chin in her hand and waited as Misty approached in the darkness of the pre-dawn. 'I've just set up and the coffee machine is almost ready.'

'That's okay. I've got plenty of time and Harry—my dog—is sound asleep in my van.'

'Good. Now I wanted to tell you what a clever lady you are,' Feath said.

'Clever?'

'The whole town is talking about your sand art. The one with the pyramids was incredible. I went home to the farm and brought my girls back to the lookout so they could see it. I can't believe that you do it with just a stick. You are so talented, Misty.'

Misty shrugged. 'It's what I do and I love it.'

'But isn't it sad when the tide comes in and washes it away? Do you take a photo of it every day from above when you're finished? I got some great shots with my phone and I saw that some of the locals are starting to post photos on Facebook and Insta. You're the talk of the town.'

'I don't want to be. And no, it doesn't make me sad when it washes away. I guess it shows everyone how ephemeral life is.'

'Ephemeral?'

'Short-lasting. Like a flower that only lives one day. It teaches us to appreciate what we have and live every day as though it is the last. We live in the moment, and enjoy the present.'

'I love that.' But Feath's gaze was shrewd. 'You've had some sadness, haven't you?'

'I have, but life goes on and we live each day to the fullest. Tell me about your girls.'

Feath rolled her eyes. 'I have two teenagers and one almost there. Sometimes I don't think I'll survive it, but I have a gorgeous husband who shares the load. It was his idea that I start the coffee van, and the lovely guy gets them off to school every morning. I deal with the afternoon stuff.'

'Sounds like you have a blessed life.'

'I do and I live in paradise too.'

'I had a little girl for a short time, but she got sick, and life was too much for her. She let go and I think of her every day when I watch the sunrise. We greet the day together. I haven't missed a day in four years.'

'Oh, sweetie. I'm so sorry.' The coffee machine clicked and Feath brushed away a tear before she picked up a mug. 'I'll put your chai in a real mug for you today. When are you moving on?'

Misty bit her lip. As much as logic was telling her it was time to leave, her heart was holding her back. It was the first time she'd felt like this and she was listening to her emotions. Someone here needed her, and until she knew who or what it was, she would stay.

'Not for a while yet.'

'I'm pleased to hear that. I'll look forward to seeing you tomorrow. Oh, and the boys have already been and gone.'

'The boys?'

'Alex and crew. They've gone down to the beach. Apparently, it's a record haul this year. Oh, here comes the fisher crew.' Misty looked up as three utes turned into the park

'Thank you, Feath. I'll see you tomorrow. And thanks for the real mug too.'

'You take care, lovely.'

Misty tiptoed to her van and peeked in. She'd left a low light on inside the door. Harry was still in doggy dreamland.

She slipped away and strolled down the hill to the lookout. The table and the lookout were in darkness and she missed the fellas as Angus had called them. She wondered if he would come today. Yesterday had been a bit tense between them for a while.

Misty knew deep down that Angus was the one who needed some help, but until he talked to her, she wouldn't intrude. She'd picked up his irritation yesterday.

What would be, would be.

Chapter 7

Angus

Wednesday

Angus was looking forward to seeing Misty this morning. He decided to walk to the lookout as he'd woken early and after the day in the office yesterday and the events at home last night, he'd had trouble sleeping.

As he'd known, Mrs Ryan had been devastated to hear that he could do nothing about the challenge to her husband's will. The outcome was going to leave her with scant funds, and his heart had gone out to her as she'd dabbed at her eyes with a lace handkerchief.

'At least one of my daughters wants to mend bridges between us,' she had said with a sob.

'That's one positive out of this whole sorry mess. I'll just have to learn to be a little bit more careful with what I have left.'

Angus had taken her down to the local government offices to help her get the application sorted for the aged pension.

As he'd driven her home, she'd put her hand on his arm. 'You're a good man, Angus, and you did your best, so please don't take it to heart. It's my sons who are the problem, and I am sure they'll realise one day what they've done is wrong.'

But he railed at the unfairness of the law and vowed that he would lobby to have it changed. Then when he'd gone home from work at five, he'd been taken aback to see Becky Barber sitting on the front porch with a sullen-looking Sean.

He still didn't know what was happening there.

If Sean hadn't broken off his engagement with Becky after the accident, Angus wouldn't feel responsible for his brother's care, and he knew he would have moved away from Snapper Bay.

Oh, he loved the place, and he loved the community that he lived in, but he wanted to see more, he thought as he strode towards the lookout.

He needed to get away, but while Sean stayed as he was, there was no chance of that happening.

His heart lifted as he approached the lookout and saw Misty silhouetted against the pink sky. For a moment he'd thought there was no one there. The table was in darkness, and the fellas weren't here this morning.

Alex had told him about Misty's sand art, and he'd gone for a walk on the beach before he'd cooked dinner last night. A solo dinner as usual.

Sean had wheeled through the house and ignored him when Angus had called him to say dinner was on the table.

Misty's artwork on the beach had been inspirational. A circle about twenty metres in diameter with scrolls and circles and smiling suns. It was hard to believe she'd used a stick to create it. It had made him feel happy, and then when he'd thought of the tide coming in and washing it away, he'd been sad.

Misty turned as he approached the timber platform.

'Hello,' she said.

'Good morning.'

'Where's your car?' She looked past him.

'I decided to walk this morning. Clear a few cobwebs.'

'It's a lovely morning for it.'

Angus nodded. 'It is, but I needed my jacket.'

'Do you live far away?'

'Did you see the hill with the water tower that has the mural?'

'I did. On the way in. I haven't started the car since I arrived.'

'We live a couple of houses down from the tower.' He sensed her withdrawal. 'My brother and I.'

'Oh.'

'Yes, we still live in the family house. Hard

to believe at thirty-five I still live in the same house I was born in. A bit boring for someone who travels, I'd say.'

'No, I think it's wonderful that you have created ties with your community and you're giving back to it with your work.'

'I might sound like a saint, but I'd give anything to be able to leave.'

'Is that your long story you mentioned the other day?'

He nodded. 'It is.'

'You look sad sometimes.'

'I've been sad for three years,' Angus said, and his attempt at a chuckle failed. 'Ever since I got trapped in Snapper Bay.'

Misty leaned back on the railing and looked at him in the dim light. 'How can you be trapped?'

'Have you got time for a short version of a long story? That is, if you're interested?'

'I have.'

***

Misty could hear the despair in Angus's voice. 'Do you want to go and sit over at the table?' she asked.

'I'm happy here. I'd hate you to miss your sunrise. Are you sure you want to be an ear?'

'I am.' She smiled at Angus and tried to let go of the compulsion to put her arms around him. He looked so sad. 'I make a very good ear.'

He moved across to stand by her and even though they weren't touching, Misty could feel his warmth. From his expression, she guessed he was feeling her presence too.

'Just over three years ago, I had an overseas trip booked. It was just before COVID and in one way it was probably good that I had to cancel it because I might have got stuck overseas.'

He cleared his throat and paused. Misty waited.

'Sean was getting married, and he was having a buck's night in Swamp Bay.'

'Swamp Bay? That's the town upriver?'

'It is. About fifteen ks up the valley. I

wanted us to get a room there but Sean wanted to come home, so I didn't drink. It didn't bother me because I'm not much of a drinker. It was a good night. A happy night. Even Alex and the fellas came.'

Angus's short clipped sentences gave away his tension. Misty moved closer and put one hand on his.

'If you don't want to keep going that's fine.'

'No, I need to talk. It feels good. Everyone here thinks they know what happened, but Sean and I are the only ones who do. It'll be good to talk it out.'

'Was it a car accident?'

'It was. He took my keys from my jacket pocket when I went to the gents as we were about to leave. Everyone else had gone and we'd stayed back to help clean up, and pay for the drinks and meals. It was just after midnight. I came out to the bar and I couldn't see him, so I grabbed my jacket off the chair and I knew straight away what he was doing.'

'He drove the car?'

Angus nodded. 'Sean is a lot younger than me. He's always been strong-minded; he and Dad used to go head to head. I was the peacekeeper and he hated that. I have no idea why he decided to drive that night. Or whether he intended to leave me there to try to find my own way home. I walked outside just as he took off in my car. In those days I only had a little Nissan hatchback and when he hit the telegraph pole up the road about half a kilometre, it just crumpled.' His breath was coming in short pants now.

Misty slipped her arms around his waist without thinking; she just followed her heart. 'Take it slow.'

Angus rested his head on her shoulder. 'I ran and it was like one of those dreams where you think you're never going to get there. There was no one else around, and I knew it wasn't good. I pulled my phone out and called triple zero. As I got there, smoke started to come out of the back of the car near the fuel tank, so I prised open the door and I dragged him out. His foot had gone through the firewall from the impact and to give you the short, short version, his leg was badly injured. They flew him to Sydney, but there was too much damage and Sean lost half his leg.'

'And the wedding?' she asked quietly.

'Sean broke the engagement by phone from his hospital bed and cancelled the wedding. He never forgave me for rescuing him. He blames me for everything. Said he'd rather be dead than a one-legged man.'

Chapter 8

Angus felt as though a load had lifted. Nothing had changed with Sean's situation, but just talking about it helped.

'I took the blame for driving, but I know they were sceptical, but there were no witnesses to say otherwise. The last thing Sean needed was a DUI charge. He had enough to deal with.'

'Were you charged?'

'No. I was breathalysed, and when they examined the car, they discovered a bolt in the back tyre. The verdict was that the tyre had blown and pushed the car into the pole. I was cleared.'

Misty's shoulders were stiff and he realised that he had shed the load, but she'd picked up the tension.

'Thank you for listening, and please don't worry. Talking it out has made me feel better. I can cope with it.'

'But I can't understand why you're trapped. Why do you have to stay in Snapper Bay?'

'Because Sean doesn't work. He refuses to get a prosthetic leg, and he won't accept the disability pension.'

'That's very hard for you. No point saying it's unfair because he's the one who lost his leg. What about his fiancée?'

'She eventually left town. She tried for months to see him, but as I said, Sean is strong-willed. It's strange, she called me the other day. Said she was coming for a visit. When I got home from the office a couple of nights back, she was sitting on the porch with Sean. He didn't look happy and he never told me why she was there.'

'Can you talk to him?'

'Honestly?' Angus knew his voice was bleak. 'I've stopped trying. I talk, Sean yells. I give up. It's been a three-year cycle. Sometimes I don't have the energy.'

Misty moved and gripped his forearms with strong hands. 'You have to. You have to make him listen. Give him the chance to know what you want to do. And then if he won't listen, you have to follow your dream. Angus, you have one life, and at the moment, you're not living it.' Her voice shook and he knew there was a lot she wasn't saying.

'And what about your life, Misty? Living in that car with Harry, taking photos and drawing in the sand every day. What sort of life is that?'

'The life I must live.'

'Why?

'Because I won't trust my heart to anyone. I'm not worthy of it.'

'What!'

'I live my life how I want. No one has to approve or tell me what to do. No one can let me down by not loving me. No one I care about can leave me this way.'

'I think you might have a story to share?' he asked quietly.

'I do.' Her smile was sad. 'But not today. Maybe not ever. Look, the sun is coming up.'

She stepped away from him and Angus felt

the loss of her proximity keenly. Raising her camera as the sun breached the horizon, there was one click only before she lowered it.

'It's time I went back to Harry.' Her voice held more sadness than usual, and his heart went out to her.

As she turned to walk away, Angus put his hand on her arm. 'Misty, wait.'

She looked up at him, her dark eyes wide and full of pain. He leaned down and brushed his lips across her cool cheek. 'Thank you for your ear. I'm going to sit down with Sean tonight.'

'I'm pleased.'

'Will you be here tomorrow?'

'I think so. I never know from one day to the next.'

'Promise me you'll be here tomorrow. One day I'd like to sit with you and hear your story. What do you think?'

She hesitated and he closed his eyes as she reached up a hand to cup his cheek.

'I promise I'll be here tomorrow.'

Chapter 9

Wednesday night

'Don't you bloody tell me what to do.' Sean's voice reverberated around the walls of the room that Angus used for a study. Once he'd enticed Sean in there on the pretext of signing some papers, Angus had locked the door, pocketed the key and sat behind his desk.

Sean had hopped in and as usual Angus's heart broke as he watched his little brother hang onto the wall as he sought to keep his balance.

'It's about time I did. I've let you off for so long.'

'Let me off? If you hadn't pulled me from the car, I would have died and I wouldn't have to put up with this half-life. How many bloody times do I have to remind you of that? Now unlock the door and let me out.'

'No.'

Sean's face was a picture and Angus realised he should have done this a long time ago. He sent a silent thank you to Misty.

'I've made a new friend this week, and she made me realise that I need to think about my life if you won't make an effort to change yours.'

'Change it? How?' The volume of his brother's voice had dropped a little.

'I want to travel.'

'And who's going to look after me? Buy the groceries, pay the bills, cook the meals?'

'You are.'

'What?'

'You heard me.'

'I'm hearing you, but I'm not believing you.'

'Well Sean, suck it up. I'm leaving.'

'When?'

'In two weeks.' Angus just plucked a time frame out of his head. There was no way he would leave that soon, but he wanted Sean to know he was serious.

'What about the business? You can't just up and leave. Not Mr Holier-Than-Thou-Save-the-World-Local-Solicitor.'

To his shame, Angus blinked back tears. 'If I'd known how much you hated me, I would have gone a long time ago, Sean. I've probably done you a disservice.'

'I don't.' Sean lowered his head and muttered.

'Don't what?'

'I don't hate you. I hate myself.'

'I should have made you go to counselling when you came home from the hospital.'

'That's what Bec said.'

'When she was here the other night?'

Sean nodded and didn't look up.

'Why was she here?'

Sean's voice was thick. 'Because she said she can't forget me. Reckons she loves me.' He looked up and gestured roughly to the stump of his leg. 'How can she love half a man?'

Tears rolled silently down Sean's cheeks, and Angus swallowed back his grief. He stood and moved around the desk and crouched in front of his brother. 'Mate. I love you, and it makes me feel so bad that I haven't helped you more.'

'How much more could you have helped me?' Sean grated out. 'Keeping a roof over my head, putting food on the table, keeping the house clean, the lawn mowed, and going to work every day. But most of all, putting up with the shit I've been.'

He leaned forward and put his head on Angus's shoulder and Angus held his brother as he cried.

Chapter 10

A month later

Misty turned with a smile as Angus stepped onto the timber platform. She held out her hand as he walked closer and reached down and kissed her cheek, as he had done every morning since he had told her about Sean's accident.

The weather had turned cooler as the days grew shorter and winter approached. The skies were clear and the sunrises had been very special.

More special because Angus had been with her for the last thirty.

They had been alone each morning as the mullet run had ended; the old fellas were sleeping in and Feath's Mobile Coffee had moved up the valley to one of the small rural villages.

'How's Sean?' Misty asked.

The joy in Angus's face warmed her more than her mohair cardigan could.

'He's so good. I owe you so much, Misty.'

'No. You did it all. What's he up to?'

'He's had his appointment with the specialist. He'd applied for the disability pension, but best of all, he's talking about getting the boats up to scratch and starting up the business again.'

'That's wonderful news.' Misty squeezed his fingers. 'And what about Becky? Is she still around?'

'She's spent a lot of time at our place in the past month, but I think they are taking it slowly. Building up trust again.'

'That's important.'

To her surprise, Angus looped his arms around her waist. 'It's very important. Do you trust me, Misty?'

She closed her eyes. She had known this moment would come because he was such a good man. Over the past month, she had enjoyed every second of his company, but she had fought the need to be with him.

Yes, she trusted him, but she didn't trust herself. If she was left again, she didn't know how she would survive the grief. She had built up a new life, but it was lonely.

I won't be tempted.

But that deep voice persisted and those arms pulled her close to a warm chest.

'I haven't pushed you, Misty, because I sensed you might leave in the dark of the night, and I wasn't prepared to lose you, but I think it's time you told me your story.'

Misty let out a soft sigh. 'Really?'

'Yes. You must know that you have become important to me. I don't want you to leave, but I know you will, and if you do . . . '

'If I do?

'I want to come with you.'

Joy blossomed in her heart, and for the first time in a long time, she let the little tendril of hope unfurl.

'Tell me your story, love.'

She moved out of his arms and turned to face the lightening sky. 'It is a very short story. I had a little girl. A gorgeous little baby who grew into a sweet little toddler. Her name was Laina.' Her voice trembled and she swallowed. 'She got sick and died, and she's seen the sun in with me every morning since I left her little body in that hospital.'

Misty tensed as Angus stepped behind her and put his arms around her. After a moment, she relaxed and leaned back against his hard chest.

'What about her father?' he asked quietly.

'Joel left me that morning too. He said he was only with me because of Laina.' She reached up, surprised to feel the wetness on her cheeks. 'I don't cry. I shouldn't be crying.'

'It's all right to cry.'

'No it's weakness and I can't be weak. Because there is just me. I can't trust. I don't want to be loved and left again. My mum and dad died, my sweet Laina died, and Joel left me. I'm not strong enough to do it again.'

'What about if someone loved you so much they couldn't imagine you not being in their life?' His arms tightened around her, and she held her breath.

'Who would that be?'

'I know it's only been a short time, Misty, but I love you. I don't want you to leave. Will you stay here for the winter?'

She shook her head. 'No, I have to follow the sun.'

He turned her gently so she was facing him. The expression in his eyes held a love that she'd never seen before. Misty forgot about her camera sitting on the railing, and she forgot about the approaching sunrise. With a shaking hand, she reached up and traced her finger around his beautiful mouth.

'You love me?'

'I love you, and I want to watch the sunrise with you every morning. I want to spend my days with you and watch the sunset each evening, and I want to spend my nights with you.'

Misty stood on her tiptoes, and when their lips met, the promise of their future was sealed.

Epilogue

One month later

Harry yapped when Sean and Becky walked to the gate in front of Angus and Sean's family home. Misty hid a smile as Angus backed out of her Coaster. No matter how hard he'd tried to persuade her, she had refused to let him buy a new van.

'You want to come with me, we do it my way,' she'd said with a laugh as they lay in the back of the van the morning they had first kissed. Angus had been late to work that day, and he'd gotten used to her small double bed over the past four weeks as he'd wound up his affairs, hired a locum, and packed for his new life with Misty.

Sean let go of Becky's hand and he walked over to the van where Angus stood scratching his head. Sean's grin was wide as he turned to Misty. 'Never in million years did I think my brother would head off in a Coaster van. The best part is, I get to mind the Audi!'

Becky caught up to Sean and linked her arm through his. 'I think it's true love. Speaking of which, let's share our news before this pair drive off into the sunset.

Angus stared and Misty smiled as Becky held out her left hand and an engagement ring flashed in the morning sunlight.

'Oh, I am so happy for you both,' she cried, reaching out first to hug Becky and then Sean.

Angus stood beside her and held out his hand to his brother, but Sean ignored it and stepped forward confidently on two feet, wrapping his arms around his big brother in a bear hug.

'You guys make sure you keep in touch and promise you'll come back for the wedding.'

Misty swallowed the lump in her throat as she watched Angus blink away tears as he thumped his brother's back. 'Wouldn't miss it for the world, would we, Misty?'

'No, we wouldn't.'

Angus let go of Sean and held his hand out

to take Misty's. 'Harry's in pride of place, the van's packed and we're right to go. Are you ready to leave, my love?'

A huge wave of love for this wonderful man rolled over Misty. She knew Angus would never let her down.

'Let's go follow the sun,' she said.

THE END

BOOKS by ANNIE SEATON

Whitsunday Dawn

Undara

Osprey Reef

 East of Alice (Nov 22)

Porter Sisters Series

Kakadu Sunset

Daintree

Diamond Sky

Hidden Valley

Larapinta

Augathella Girls Series

Outback Roads

Outback Sky

Outback Escape

Outback Wind

Pentecost Island Series

Pippa

Eliza

Nell

Tamsin

Evie

Cherry

Odessa

Sienna

Tess

Isla

Sunshine Coast Series

Waiting for Ana

The Trouble with Jack

Healing His Heart

Sunshine Coast Boxed Set

Richards Brother Series

The Trouble with Paradise
Marry in Haste
Outback Sunrise

Bondi Beach Love Series

Beach House

Beach Music

Beach Walk

Beach Dreams

The House on the Hill

Second Chance Bay Series

<u>Her Outback Playboy</u>

<u>Her Outback Protector</u>

<u>Her Outback Haven</u>

<u>Her Outback Paradise</u>

<u>The McDougalls of Second Chance Bay Boxed Set</u>

Love Across Time Series

<u>Come Back to Me</u>

<u>Follow Me</u>

<u>Finding Home</u>

<u>The Threads that Bind</u>

Others

<u>The Trouble with Paradise</u>

<u>Deadly Secrets</u>

Adventures in Time

Silver Valley Witch

The Emerald Necklace

Worth the Wait

 Ten Days in Paradise

Follow the Sun (May 22)

Secrets of River Cottage (Nov 22)

BOOKS BY SUSANNE BELLAMY

Rural fiction

Hearts of the Outback (6 book series)

Individual titles – Hearts of the Outback

FOUR SEASONS SHORT AND SWEET

Just One Kiss

Heartbreak Homestead

Long Way Home

Winds of Change

Wild About Harry

The Cattleman's Promise

Home to Lark Creek

A Promise of Home

Hard Road Home

Turn Left for Home

Home from the Hill - Finalist – RWA RuBY Award 2021

Bindarra Creek Romance

Second Chance Love

FOUR SEASONS SHORT AND SWEET

<u>Pearls and Green Beer</u> (novella)

<u>In the Heat of the Night</u>

<u>Forgotten Secrets</u> (14 August 2022)

<u>Through Escape Publishing</u>

<u>Starting Over</u> (Also appears in print bind up: *Heart of the Town* - four book anthology)

<u>Engaging the Enemy</u>

<u>Her Christmas Kisses</u> (Also appears in print: Christmas Among the Gum Trees)

<u>Contemporary romance</u>:

<u>White Ginger</u> (Finalist – RWA Emerald Award)

<u>Romantic suspense</u>:

<u>The Emerald Lei</u> (originally published as *Winning the*

321

Heiress' Heart)

High Stakes (A High Stakes Novel book 1) *

 Singapore Trap (A High Stakes Novel book 2)

High Stakes Book 3 coming - 2023

Novellas:

A Taste of Christmas (4 authors in A Season to Remember)

One Night in Tuscany

When You Wish

Second Chance Cafe

Regency:

A Spy for Lady Clementine

Spying for the Earl

FOUR SEASONS SHORT AND SWEET

<u>Sweet Secrets of Swain Cove</u> (November 2022)

<u>Ransom Women</u> (**New series starting 4 July 2022)

<u>Under the Dark Moon</u>

<u>Under the Same Stars (Jan 2023 release)</u>

About the Authors

Annie Seaton

Annie lives in Australia, on the beautiful north coast of New South Wales. She sits in her writing chair and looks out over the tranquil Pacific Ocean. She writes contemporary romance and loves telling the stories that always have a happily ever after. She lives with her very own hero of many years and they share their home with Toby, the naughtiest dog in the universe, and Barney, the ragdoll kitten, who hides when the four grandchildren come to visit.

Stay up to date with her latest releases at her website: http://www.annieseaton.net

If you would like to stay up to date with Annie's releases, subscribe to her newsletter here: http://www.annieseaton.net

Susanne Bellamy

Born and raised in Toowoomba, Susanne is an Australian author of contemporary and rural romances set in Australia and exotic locations. She adores travel with her husband, both at home and overseas (and hopes to do more one day when the world opens up again).

Her heroes have to be pretty special to live up to her real life hero. He saved her life then married her.

She is published with Harlequin Mira/Escape, and has written several self-published rural series. A popular guest speaker, she has been invited to speak in libraries, book clubs, and to community groups.

You can find Susanne at

http://www.susannebellamy.com